THE CHRISTMAS CRAFT FAIR CAPER

A COZY QUILTS CLUB MYSTERY
BOOK 6

MARSHA DEFILIPPO

To get the latest information on new releases, excerpts and more, be sure to sign up for Marsha's newsletter.

https://marshadefilippo.com/newsletter

Dedicated to
Eleanor P.. Heath,
who always wanted to be a published author.
This one's for you, Grammie.

CONTENTS

CHAPTER 1

"Can you believe the craft fair is next Saturday? How is everyone coming along with your projects?" Annalise Jordan asked without waiting for a reply to her first question.

She was one of four women who were members of The Cozy Quilts Club, now gathered at Eva Perkins's home for their weekly meeting. Eva had embraced the holiday season with decorations in every room inside her house, and the evergreens in her front yard had been strung with lights. The woodsy scent of a real Christmas tree in her living room, along with cinnamon scented candles, added to the mood.

Annalise had presented the idea of participating at Glen Lake's first annual Christmas craft fair a few weeks earlier and they had agreed to rent a table. It was being put on by the town's Recreation Department as a fundraiser for the summer camp programs held for children who were residents of Glen Lake.

"I've got about a dozen mug rugs finished," Sarah Pascal replied. "Thank you again for donating the fabric, Eva. It's saved me a lot of shopping time, not to mention the cost of the material. The one with the Christmas trees on the dark green background was my favorite."

"It was my pleasure. Besides, now I won't feel as guilty if I buy some more," Eva said and winked.

"Haven't we spoken about this? No more fabric until you've used up your stash!" Annalise said, a stern expression on her face.

"Yes, ma'am," she replied, but they both broke out in grins.

"I've been making table runners but I've only finished six so far. The material you donated is working up so nicely, I'm tempted to keep one of them for myself," Jennifer Ryder added.

"I have more of it left if you decide to make one after the craft fair is over, Jen. I've got two tree skirts, four wine bags, and six stockings. That's the beauty of being retired and single. It gives me a lot of extra time to spend at the sewing machine. Jim may be feeling a little neglected, but I'll make it up to him later. I had a few things I'd stitched up when I first stopped working and thought about having an Etsy shop, but changed my mind. They're not made with holiday fabric, but that might work in our favor. Not everyone is going to want just holiday items, so I'll bring those, too."

Eva was a retired schoolteacher and lived alone with her cat, Reuben, but was also in a relationship with Jim Davis, a former state police officer.

"That's impressive, everyone! I've been making fabric gift box covers. I've made three different sizes that fit the boxes you can buy. The covers are made like an envelope and you just slip the box inside."

"You might already have a customer with me, Lise. That would make gift wrapping so much easier and wouldn't require stuffing a bag with tissue paper. Ashley is famous… infamous might be a better word… for peeking in gift bags. She might not be as tempted if she had to do more than look in a bag," Sarah said, referring to her wife.

"I think this is a great start, especially considering the short notice we had to work on them. Luckily, I had a light schedule this week," Annalise said. Although she could be retired, she worked from home as a Reiki practitioner and was able to set her own hours. "By the time the fair starts, we should have enough projects for the first weekend," she said, holding up her right hand with her fingers crossed.

"Don't forget we'll each need to donate an item for the silent auction," Jennifer reminded them.

"I spoke with Bethany Cox. She's the director of the Rec Department and the organizer for the event," Annalise said for Sarah's benefit. The other ladies lived in Glen Lake, but Sarah lived in nearby Bangor. "They've been able to gather enough banquet tables so no one will have to bring their own, but we'll need to provide our own table covering if we want one. The tables are only six feet long but should be plenty of space for the items we'll have on the opening day. I was thinking it would be nice to have a banner to drape over the front with Cozy Quilts Club appliqued on it."

"That's a great idea, Annalise! I can do that unless anyone else wants to take it on," Eva said.

"No argument from me!" Jennifer said. "Or me," Annalise and Sarah said in unison.

"I already have credit card payment equipment that I use for my business and could set it up to take payments for our crafts," Annalise volunteered. "Chances are not everyone will have cash and I think it best if we don't take checks. These days most people use their debit or credit cards, anyway."

"Perfect! We should probably bring some cash for change, too, though," Jennifer said.

"So many details that never occurred to me!" Eva said.

"By the time the fair is over, we'll be experts," Annalise said, smiling. "I have one other thing to suggest, but I'd understand if you think it's too much."

The ladies eyed her warily.

"What if we all wore ugly Christmas sweaters?" she asked, and held her breath.

The other three women stared at each other with nearly identical expressions. They all had their eyebrows raised in surprise. Eva was the first to break the awkward silence when she guffawed, and the others broke out in smiles.

"I'm game even if you don't want to," she directed at Jennifer and Sarah.

"I already have one, so I'll play along," Jennifer said.

Sarah was the last to speak. "If everybody else is okay with it, I'll do it, too."

Annalise clapped her hands. "This is going to be fun. Does anyone have any other suggestions or thought of something I've forgotten?"

They each looked from one to the other, but no one spoke at first.

"I can't think of anything now, but I reserve the right to ask later. We might have more suggestions after the first day. It seems there's always something you've forgotten or didn't think about until after the fact," Jennifer said.

"Okay, in that case, meeting adjourned?" Eva asked.

"Can you believe we had a meeting that was all about sewing and no discussion about solving a murder?" Sarah asked.

The ladies were not only quilters but over the months since they formed the club, they had also been part of the investigations into several murders. Their amateur sleuth skills, that included using paranormal abilities each of them possessed, came to light when Jennifer's great-aunt had been murdered. Since then, homicide detectives, Phil Roberts and Dennis Smith, found their help invaluable in cracking that case and four others to assist them in bringing the killers to justice. It had taken a huge leap of faith on their part to accept that the women were telling the truth about their abilities and not perpetrating a hoax.

"As far as I'm concerned, that's a good thing!" Annalise replied to Sarah's question. "Knock on wood it won't be the exception instead of the rule."

"I'll second that!" Eva said and was rewarded with three heads nodding their assent.

CHAPTER 2

The Glen Lake Elementary School cafeteria, usually empty on a Saturday, was abuzz with activity when Annalise, Eva, Sarah, and Jennifer arrived. Volunteers were still setting up the last of the banquet tables for the vendors and the sounds of chatter and laughter filled the room. One corner of the room had been decorated with an imitation Christmas tree and a comfy chair was set up in front of it. Teenagers dressed in elf costumes and placing wrapped gift boxes, which were probably empty, under the tree, were a clue that the chair was intended for Santa Claus. Others were hanging decorations and garlands of popcorn on the tree. A huge banner was displayed on one wall announcing Glen Lake's First Annual Christmas Craft Fair. Christmas music piped through the room's speakers added to the jolly atmosphere. A middle-aged woman holding a clipboard approached them as they waited just inside the entrance to the cafeteria, unsure where they should go.

"You made it!" she said, her enthusiasm, despite the chaos behind her, shining through.

Annalise spoke first as their unofficial leader. "We did. You'd never know this is a cafeteria. The decorations are so festive, Bethany! They should really put everyone in a holiday mood."

Bethany beamed at the praise. "The volunteers have done a great job. I hope they're still feeling as excited when it comes time to take everything down and do it all over again every weekend for the next two weeks."

"If there's anything we can do to help out, just let us know," Eva said.

"Thanks, I appreciate the offer. In the meantime, though, let's get you set up at your table. Let me see," she said checking her clipboard. "Here you are. You're in space six. The tables are marked, but it's one of the ones under the banner."

Another vendor entered, catching Bethany's attention. "Unless you need anything else, I should go check in the others."

"We're all set, Bethany," Annalise said and walked toward the table assigned to them with the others following behind. "Not this one," she said when they reached the tables Bethany had directed them to.

"That leaves this one," Jennifer said, moving over to the one next to it.

There were ten in all, and had been set up in a U-shape around the perimeter. The Santa display had been placed at the far end of the room. It was slightly away from the vendors but close enough to encourage shoppers to check out their wares once the little ones had visited Santa and told him what they wanted for Christmas.

"I've got the tablecloth and our banner right here," Eva said, pulling it out of a bag in her rolling cart. She shook out the table-cloth and Jennifer helped her arrange it on the table. Once the banner had been laid over the tablecloth, they all took a moment to inspect Eva's handiwork. The words Cozy Quilts Club had been cut out of different fabrics in large block stencil style and appliquéd to the background giving them a colorful, scrappy appearance.

"You did a great job, Eva. It looks terrific!" Sarah told her.

"I'm pretty pleased with it, if I do say so myself," Eva said, her face glowing with pride. "Enough admiration for now. Let's get the rest of this set up."

"I brought a few decorations for our display, too." Jennifer began pulling things out of her bag and placing them on the table. "I've got wrapped candy canes for anyone who wants one. I found a string of battery-operated Christmas lights to run across the front of the table and a little artificial Christmas tree. Unless you think it's too much," she said after seeing their expressions. They all had their mouths slightly open in surprise as they surveyed her accessories.

"Not at all, Jen. I don't know why I didn't think of any of this myself. My focus was all on what we have to sell, but this will be the extra touch that will bring people to our table," Annalise said. "Hand me one end of the lights and I'll spread it out to the other side of the table."

They all pitched in to decorate the table and set up their display of items for sale and then took seats in the folding chairs left for them by the volunteers to wait for the fair to open to the public.

"Oh, look, that's Fiona Walsh. She makes the most beautiful knit and crochet clothing. I'm going to check out her display later. She might have something I need for my gift list." Eva said.

"That never even occurred to me. I might be able to finish all my holiday shopping right here. That would make my life so much easier!" Sarah said, her voice wistful. "And then I'll know what sizes I'll need to buy for your box covers, Annalise."

"We could take turns watching our table so each of us can look around," Jennifer suggested.

"It's a deal," Annalise said.

Their curiosity was piqued as other vendors arrived to set up their displays.

"Do you know any of the other vendors?" Sarah asked.

"Not all of them, but the quilter is Abigail Adams. She wins awards for her quilts. Bethany told me Liam Campbell is the one with the pottery. The artist with the watercolors is Sophia Peterson. I'm a little surprised she's doing this. She has paintings in art galleries on the coast that sell for thousands of dollars but maybe she brought more affordable ones for this. I'm not sure about the others," Annalise said.

"Vanessa Barnes makes the jewelry. That's Penelope Butler next to her. She's a weaver. Quentin Gray does the woodworking and Nathan Cooper is at the table next to us. He does the stained glass. Willow Stone is in between them. She makes gorgeous art paper," Jennifer picked up where Annalise left off.

"And all of these people live in Glen Lake?" Sarah asked, incredulously.

"They do," Jennifer replied.

"I had no idea we had so many talented artists in the town," Eva said. "I'm a little self-conscious now about my stuff compared to theirs."

"You shouldn't be, Eva. What we brought may not be gallery level work, but we made each thing with care and the real reason we're here is to help support the fundraiser," Annalise said.

"You're right. We're all contributing to the event in whatever way we can. It sounds like the doors have opened for the public, so we'll see how it goes. It looks like Santa will have his lap full." Eva nodded her head at the line of children and parents queueing up for their turn, and then did a double take. "Wait a minute. Is that Jim under that beard?" She turned to the others, her eyes round with surprise.

They all looked in that direction and a smile crossed their faces as they recognized him, too.

"He didn't tell you he was doing this?" Jennifer asked.

"No! I had no idea. Just wait until I talk to him later," Eva said, but she was smiling, too.

The room filled with the sounds of crowd noises and the next two hours flew by as eager shoppers arrived and bought their goods.

At last, there was a lull in the steady stream of shoppers stopping at their table and Sarah was about to take a break to check out the other vendors for her own shopping when Bethany Cox approached. She was walking with a tall, thin man in his fifties carrying a digital camera.

"I've been waiting for an opportunity to come over so I can introduce you to Benjamin Brooks. He's a professional photographer and he's doing a book about craft fairs around the country," Bethany explained.

"A pleasure to meet you," he said and extended his hand to Sarah who introduced herself and he moved on to the others who repeated the process.

"I saw you earlier taking photos at some of the other tables but I thought you must be here from The Bangor News," Annalise said.

"No, I'm here on my own but I'm surprised they didn't send a photographer out. You've drawn a good crowd for your event. As Bethany said, I'm working on a book about craft fairs, primarily those in small towns. My focus is on how they provide opportunities for rural craft artisans to exhibit their work. Would you mind if I took your pictures for my book? I can do a group photo if you'd prefer."

They turned to each other and shrugged their shoulders in mutual agreement to their unspoken question about whether it was okay.

"Sure," Annalise said.

"That's great! If you would stand over here so that I have you centered with your banner."

They moved in closer together toward the middle of the table and he snapped several photos. He took a business card out of his pocket and handed it to Annalise. "That has my email address on it. Would you mind sending me the contact information for each of you? I'll need to have official permissions for the publisher to use your photos in my book. They'll be the ones to send the forms to you, but by the time they get around to that, I'll have moved on to another town."

"Of course," Annalise said, taking the card and placing it in the zippered pouch she'd brought, filled with cash to make change.

When he walked away, Annalise turned to Eva. "Did you hear that? He called us rural craft artisans. I told you that you didn't have to be self-conscious about what you've made."

Eva started to protest, but squared her shoulders and stood taller instead. "You're right, he did. Rural craft artisan. I like the sound of that."

"If it's okay, I'm going to walk around to see if I can find gifts to buy to cross off my Christmas list," Sarah said. "I was just about to do that when they came over."

"Go right ahead. The crowd has thinned out so we should be fine. I'd like to take a turn when you come back," Jennifer said, looking to the others.n

"Fine by me," Eva said. "I can wait until tomorrow to check out Fiona's table. I'm sure she'll still have more things to sell."

"Me, too," Annalise agreed. "I'd like to check out what the others have but I don't have to do it today."

As Sarah walked away, Annalise's attention was drawn to Fiona Walsh's table where a woman she didn't recognize, wearing a floppy hat that obscured her face, was standing with her back toward Annalise. Their voices were too low to make out what they were saying but the tension between them was unmistakable in their body language. When a potential customer walked toward Fiona's table, the woman left and Fiona's gaze followed her, her eyes hard and her mouth set in a thin line. As soon as the woman had left the room, Fiona's dour expression morphed into a broad smile as she welcomed the customer to her table.

Hmmm, that was interesting, Annalise thought as she filed the exchange away in her mind but didn't have time to discuss it with the others because the next wave of shoppers arrived at their table.

CHAPTER 3

"What did Jim have to say for himself?" Jennifer asked Eva the next day when they were setting up their display.

Eva chuckled. "He told me he figured that would be the only way we'd spend time together until the craft fair is over. He was teasing, but I was right when I said that I'll have to make it up to him once this is over." She glanced up from laying her items on the table as she felt eyes on her. "Speak of the devil," she said, smiling and waving at Jim a/k/a Santa Claus, who winked at her in reply.

"Where's Annalise?" Sarah asked.

"I think she was talking to Bethany," Jennifer said, looking up and surveying the room. "There she is over by Abigail's table. Looks like she's done," she said when she saw Annalise had ended her conversation with Bethany and was walking toward their table.

"The photographer gave me the idea to talk to Bethany about contacting The Bangor News to run a story about the craft fair and fundraiser. I gave her Susan Reynold's contact info. Susan might not be interested but she might know someone else on staff who would," Annalise explained.

"That was thoughtful of you," Eva said.

"I was worried she would think I was butting in, but she seemed appreciative."

"We still have two more weekends so it's not too late to promote it. One of the local TV stations might be interested in doing a spot for it, too," Jennifer added.

It only took half the time to set up their table display this time which left them time to spare before the doors opened to the public.

"If you don't mind, I'd like to take a look around to see what the other vendors have. I didn't have time to do that yesterday. By the end of the day, I was too exhausted," Annalise said.

"I don't have a problem with that. Take your time," Eva replied.

"Me, either," Jennifer said.

"I got to do my shopping yesterday, so I'm all set," Sarah chimed in.

Annalise started with the vendor's tables to their left. At the first table was the jewelry artisan, Vanessa Barnes, whose work included both high-end jewelry with genuine gemstones and silver and gold settings as well as more affordable pieces.

"Your designs are beautiful. There's something to be said for the elegance of simplicity, especially in these pieces. Did you learn to do the silversmithing on your own or did you take classes?"

"A little of both," the thirty-something, tall redhead, said. "I've loved jewelry ever since I was a little girl. My mom had to hide her good pieces when I was really little or she'd find me wearing them while I was playing outside."

Annalise returned her smile, imagining the scene.

"When I was older, I started making my own pieces, but I wasn't satisfied with using the supplies you find in the local craft store, so I researched where to take classes. I was lucky enough to find a local artist who was willing to teach me what I couldn't learn through books and online videos. And the rest is history."

Annalise spotted a pair of earrings with tear-drop shaped amethysts set in silver.

"Oh, I love these! If you haven't sold them by the time the fair is over, I'll take them."

"Would you like me to set them aside for you?"

"No, if someone else wants them, it wasn't meant to be for me. I'll be back later to check but I want to browse what the other vendors have before the doors open."

No one was currently manning the next table, but she admired the handwoven linens on display. She had grown up with the artist, Penelope "Penny" Butler. They were kindred spirits with their eclectic styles. She had also grown up with Fiona Walsh, who she'd seen yesterday with the woman wearing the floppy hat, at the next booth. Fiona was frantically rummaging through her tote behind the table.

"Are you okay, Fiona?" Annalise asked.

Fiona startled and looked up with a distracted expression on her face.

"I'm missing some of my things. They were in my tote last night when I left and I kept track of everything I sold yesterday, so I'm positive they should still be here. I was told it would be safe to leave my things, but obviously it wasn't."

The irritation in her voice was unmistakable.

"Have you spoken to Bethany about this?"

"Not yet, but you can bet I will."

Fiona jammed the lid down on the tote and stormed off. Even though the negative energy wasn't directed at her, the exchange unsettled Annalise to the point that she decided to return to the club's table and center herself before the shoppers arrived.

"Are you okay?" Eva asked, seeing Annalise's expression.

"I just need a few minutes to pull myself together."

"What happened?"

"Fiona told me some of her things were missing. She was pretty upset about it and is going to talk to Bethany. She was having what looked like a heated discussion with someone yesterday."

"Do you think that person had something to do with this?"

"It seems like a possibility. I'm going to sit quietly for a few minutes and see if I can get any impressions."

Eva nodded, understanding that by impressions, Annalise meant she intended to use her psychic skills to find an answer.

"If you need to go someplace where you'll have less distractions, we can hold down the fort. We've still got about a half hour before people will start coming in."

"Thanks. I think I will do that. I can sit in my car and I'll set an alarm for myself in case I lose track of time."

"Is Annalise okay? She looks like she's on a mission," Jennifer asked after she'd walked away.

"She needs to clear her mind. Fiona Walsh told her she'd had things stolen overnight and it upset her. She'll be back in time before the doors open."

"Someone stole things?" Sarah asked. The inflection in her voice conveying her surprise.

"I can't believe it either. Annalise saw Fiona arguing with someone yesterday. There's a possibility it could be someone who was being spiteful."

"I hope that's all it was," Jennifer said.

"Me, too. But let's think positively it will all be resolved. We don't want to start the day on a negative note."

"You're right," Jennifer said, smiling, but couldn't completely shake the unsettled sensation this had cast over the day.

Annalise sat in her car and closed her eyes. The sounds of cars coming in and out of the parking lot and the chatter of people talking as they walked into the building or back to their cars, thwarted all her attempts to focus and she finally gave up.

"Anything?" Eva asked when she returned to the table.

"No, I couldn't concentrate. I'll try later."

———

"I don't think we had a chance to take a breath today! It was even busier than yesterday," Eva said when the fair closed for the day four hours later.

"I know! I'm completely sold out of what I brought. It's a good thing we've got a week before the next one so I can make more," Sarah said.

"Me, too," Jennifer and Annalise agreed.

"How about you, Nathan?" Eva asked the gentleman manning the table next to them.

"I did okay. I wasn't sure if stained glass items would be a seller but I've sold out of all the tree ornaments and holiday-themed night lights."

"Oh, no! Will you be making more to bring next week? I was hoping to buy some of the ornaments, but never got a chance to visit your table." Annalise's face drooped with disappointment.

"Absolutely! They were too big a seller to not bring more. Tell you what, next week you come see me before the doors open and you can have first pick," Nathan said, giving her a comforting smile.

Annalise's face brightened and she returned his smile. "It's a deal!"

"Well, the plus side of selling out is that we don't have much to pack to take home," Jennifer said.

"You've got that right. I'm already done," Eva said. "Unless anyone needs my help, I'm going to find Santa and take him to dinner at The Checkout Diner. It's part of my making up plan for abandoning him while I've been sewing."

Annalise chuckled. "I'm all set. You two have a good time and I'll catch up with you later." She glanced over at Fiona's table. Fiona's eyebrows were knit together and her lips were pursed as she carelessly tossed the items left on her table into her tote. *Something else is going on here* Annalise heard her spidey senses speak inside her head.

CHAPTER 4

"It's déjà vu all over again," Annalise said when Eva and Sarah arrived the next Saturday.

"The week went by too quickly! I was afraid I wouldn't have time to make more things to bring, but I had a surge of energy Thursday and got a lot done. I'm hoping they'll last through tomorrow, though," Eva said.

"I didn't do as well," Sarah said. "A big job came in on Wednesday so I didn't have as much free time for sewing, but I've got more mug rugs. I've learned how to do them like an assembly line so it doesn't take me nearly as long. Ashley pitched in, too, and cut out the fabrics for me. That was a huge timesaver so I was able to finish more than I thought I had when I counted them up last night. "

"If we decide to do this next year, we should start making things as soon as this is done. If we do a little at a time, by this time next year, we'll have enough to last us through all three weekends without needing to make more in between," Annalise suggested.

"That would be the smart thing to do, and a lot less stressful. Plus, it would give me an excuse to buy some of the holiday fabric at Quilting Essentials when it goes on sale," Eva said.

Annalise shook her head. "You're hopeless," she teased. "But you're not wrong about buying it when it's on sale. I think I'll do the same."

"I might do that, too. I really appreciate the fabric you donated, but we've put a big dent in your stash and it would be good to mix it up with new fabrics," Sarah said.

"Here comes Jennifer. Oh, look, she's got Boscoe with her!" Annalise said and the others followed her gaze toward the door.

Jennifer had a rolling cart in one hand and the Jack Russell terrier she'd adopted after her great-aunt Sadie had been murdered, on a leash in the other. He had witnessed the murder and told Eva the killer's identity. Jennifer lived on the opposite side of the street from Sadie and they'd visited each other often which made Boscoe's transition to his new forever family much easier.

"I'm sorry I'm late. Dave needed my help tying down Santa Claus. It's one of those inflatable ones and when we woke up this morning, Santa was levitating. One of the stakes had pulled loose. We were lucky to catch it before the other stakes came out and Santa was flying without his reindeers."

"Oh, no! I'm glad you caught it in time. And don't worry about being late. You still have plenty of time to get your things set up before the doors open," Annalise said.

"Boscoe! It's so wonderful to see you!" Eva gushed, bending down to scratch the dog under his chin and his tail began to wag. Her paranormal skill was the ability to communicate with animals.

I'm happy to see you, too, Eva, he said, licking her hand and giving her a doggie smile.

"I checked with Bethany to make sure it would be alright to have him here. She said as long as I have him leashed behind the table and he doesn't bark, it would be okay. Dave and the kids were going into Bangor to do some Christmas shopping, and I didn't want to leave him alone all morning," Jennifer explained.

Annalise and Sarah gathered around the dog and each had a

turn as he basked in their attention. Jennifer set down Boscoe's dog bed and hooked the leash to her chair leg, causing him to whimper his protest. "Sorry, buddy, but I have to set up my display and we've got to follow the rules," she told him.

"It's alright, we'll be right here with you, Boscoe. You just let one of us know if you need to take a walk outside to do your business," Eva said. He gave her his best puppy dog eyes, but when it was apparent it wasn't working, he stepped onto his bed and laid down with his muzzle on his front paws and let out a big sigh of resignation.

"Hi, Nathan. I hope you didn't forget to bring the tree ornaments," Annalise said when their neighbor arrived with his wares.

"You've got first dibs as soon as I finish setting them out," he said, giving her a smile.

"Benjamin Brooks is here again," Sarah pointed to the photographer who was already taking photos of the other vendors trickling in and setting up their displays.

It wasn't long before all the tables were piled high with the vendors' craft items and the room was filled with chatter and the sound of Christmas tunes being played over the school's sound system like they had the last weekend. The elves had finished setting up Santa's display and Jim arrived in his Santa suit and fake beard, giving Eva a wink as he walked by their table.

"Did anyone have a chance to look at Abigail Adams's quilts last time? She brought some amazing quilts," Eva asked.

"I did. I'm in awe of her work and someday I hope to be her when I grow up," Jennifer said, her expression wistful as she looked toward Abigail's exhibit, eliciting chuckles from her fellow quilters.

"Good morning, ladies," a tall, handsome man in his sixties with salt and pepper hair and blue eyes said when he arrived at their table. "I'm Liam Campbell and I do the pottery," he said pointing towards his table. "I'm looking for gifts for my shopping list and was hoping you'd let me purchase some early before you've sold out."

"Of course! Please do!" Annalise said.

"Tell me a little about yourselves. Are you all from Glen Lake?"

"How about you?" Annalise asked him to make conversation after they had each introduced themselves, despite Jennifer having already told them he lived in Glen Lake.

"I moved here about two years ago. I don't usually do craft fairs but thought it was time for me to get out in the community to meet more people. I have a studio in my home and sell my pottery to gift shops so it keeps me busy on site."

"It's very nice to meet you, Liam. Welcome to Glen Lake. I'm going to make sure to visit your table before we leave today. I need to do more shopping myself," Eva said, giving him a wide grin.

Just as Liam was finishing his purchases, Bethany Cox announced that she would be opening the doors in two minutes. Noticing Benjamin standing off to the side with his camera poised, Liam turned and held up one of the stockings he'd bought from Annalise and smiled as Benjamin snapped the photo.

"I'd better go back to my table, but it was nice meeting you all. I hope we have a chance to talk more later," he said, but it was Annalise he was looking at the longest, before he turned to walk back.

Annalise's attention was on Liam as she followed him the entire time he walked away and it took a loud clearing of Eva's throat before she was able to return her focus to the others.

"Not a bad piece of scenery," Eva said, waggling her eyebrows at Annalise, making her flush a bright shade of pink at being caught.

"Oh, shush." Annalise began rearranging her display and Eva realized she had embarrassed her.

"I'm sorry. I didn't mean to embarrass you," she said quietly and put her hand on Annalise's forearm.

"It's okay." She stopped fussing with her things and looked Eva in the eyes. "I don't know what came over me. I haven't had chemistry with a man for years, but that spark definitely got lit." She looked over at Liam who was taking mugs out of a box and placing them on his table. He glanced in her direction and she quickly looked down and began rearranging again. "Darn, he caught me. Eva, I feel like a teenager," she spoke softly so the others wouldn't overhear.

"Would that be a bad thing?" Eva asked.

"Let's talk later. People are starting to come in and this isn't a conversation I want to have here."

Eva nodded her head. "I understand. Would you like to come over to my house when we're done?"

"You don't have plans with Jim?"

"Not until this evening. We could stop at The Checkout for some take-out. I didn't have any lunch planned and need to do some grocery shopping. I've spent most of my free time at the sewing machine, so my cupboards are getting bare."

"That sounds good. My treat." Annalise gave Eva a quick hug.

The constant flow of customers kept them all too busy to chat for the next couple of hours, but they finally caught a break and collapsed into their chairs, grateful to be off their feet. Eva bent down to stroke Boscoe's head when he began to whimper, which caught Annalise's attention and she followed his gaze toward Willow Stone's table. Willow's face was broken out in red blotches and it looked as though she was having trouble breathing. Annalise sat straight up and then jumped to her feet.

"Oh no! Something's wrong with Willow," she said and ran toward her. "What's wrong?" Annalise asked when she got to her table. She was scrambling through her backpack, but looked up at the sound of Annalise's voice.

"Need my Epi pen. Think someone must have peanuts. Got

it," she said and pulled it out of her purse, injecting it into her thigh.

Violet Ouellette, one of the fair volunteers rushed over to the table. "I called 911. They're on their way."

Willow only nodded her head and sat in her chair waiting for the medicine to take effect. Annalise spotted Nathan standing off to the side, wringing his hands, and looking distressed.

"Are you okay, Nathan?" she asked.

"I'm so sorry. I didn't know," he apologized, his face distraught. "I just heard you say you're allergic to peanuts. I wasn't thinking about anyone having allergies and I had a bag to snack on. I'd opened them a couple minutes ago and… I'm so sorry… I thought you had to eat them to have a reaction. I had no idea it could happen if you were just around them."

"It's okay. You didn't mean to kill me," Willow waved her hand weakly at him and smiled to reassure him she was teasing.

The sound of a siren announced the ambulance pulling into the school's parking lot and a minute later, two EMTs hurried into the cafeteria. Violet met them at the entrance and pointed to Willow. "That's her."

A small crowd of curious onlookers was gathering nearby. Violet went over to them to move them along.

"She's being taken care of so you can go back to your shopping. She doesn't need people gawking at her," she told them in a no-nonsense tone of voice, leaving no doubt she expected them to do as she said without argument.

"I used my Epi pen," Willow told the EMTs as soon as they arrived at her table.

"We'll need to check you just in case, and we should take you to the ER to make sure you'll be okay," one of them told her.

By this time Bethany Cox had arrived to join the group at Willow's table.

"I know. I'll need to pack up my things first, though," Willow told the EMT.

"Don't worry about your things, Willow. I'll pack them up for you and take them home with me if you're okay with that. You can let me know later if you're up to coming in tomorrow," Bethany told her.

"Thank you. I'd appreciate that. I should be fine tomorrow but I'll call you if I can't make it back." She picked up her back-pack and stood to leave. "I'm ready. I'll go with you in the ambu-lance but I want to walk out under my own power if you don't mind," she told the EMT who had been examining her. "It's embarrassing enough to have this happen in front of a crowd."

"Alright, but I'll be right here beside you," he told her.

Once they'd left the room, the silence that had taken over during the drama was replaced by the sounds of talking and customers resuming their shopping.

Annalise could tell that Nathan was still obsessing about the incident and he was slumped in his seat. He looked up when she approached and put her hand lightly on his shoulder.

"I didn't know…"

"Of course, you didn't. She's going to be okay. You can believe me about that," she told him. Her inner voice had spoken to her with that information as she watched the interaction between Willow and the EMT and by the time they left, Willow's aura was returning to its normal color.

"I hope so. I'll never eat peanuts in public again," he said, his voice determined.

"That's a good idea for all of us," Annalise said, smiling. She silently channeled Reiki energy toward him to take the edge off his guilt about the situation.

"I think I'm going to pack up my things now. It's nearly time for the fair to end anyway, so I hope no one will mind."

"I think they'll understand," Annalise said. "I hope you'll be back tomorrow."

"Yes, I'll be back. I just need a little time to pull myself together. Thank you for being here and being so kind."

"You're most welcome. I'd better go back to my table. Get a good night's sleep and tomorrow this will all be behind you."

She walked back to the table where her friends were watching anxiously.

"Is she okay?" Jennifer asked.

"She's going to be fine. She has a peanut allergy but Nathan didn't know that. He had a bag of peanuts to snack on and that triggered Willow's reaction." She looked back to where Bethany and Violet were packing up Willow's things. As she did, a niggling sense of something wrong overcame her, but she didn't have time now to pursue it. She made a mental note to do that when she was home again.

CHAPTER 5

"Well, that was an eventful day!" Eva said once she and Annalise were sitting at her dining room table with their take-out lunches.

"It was," Annalise replied, thoughtfully. The sensation she'd had earlier was still troubling her. "I don't think Willow's episode was as innocent as it appeared."

"What do you mean?"

"I'm not sure yet. It's just a hunch that there's something more going on than meets the eye. Do you remember I told you that Fiona Walsh said she'd had some of her things go missing?"

"I do. You think they're connected in some way?"

Annalise pressed her lips together as she thought about how to reply. "That's what's bothering me. I can't think of any reason for why they'd be connected, but still, my spidey senses are raising a red flag."

"I haven't known you that long, but in the short time I have, I've learned when you get a hunch like that, you're usually right."

"I wasn't able to concentrate with so many distractions, but I'm going to do a meditation when I'm home. Maybe it will come to me."

"Be sure to let me know tomorrow if you get any answers," Eva said.

"You'll be the first on my list," Annalise said.

"Now, let's discuss more exciting topics. Like how you were blushing like a schoolgirl when Liam Campbell looked at you," Eva said, a smug smile on her face.

Annalise let out her breath in a deep sigh.

"You didn't really think I was going to forget about that, did you?" Eva teased.

"Well, I was hoping if I didn't bring it up, you might," Annalise said, although they both knew she didn't really believe it.

"Sooooo...."

"Okay, I admit it. He made me blush. I haven't had this kind of a response to a man in... well, decades," she said, after thinking about how long it had been.

"How long has it been since your husband, Peter, died?"

"More than thirty years. I think I've mentioned before that I tried dating for a while, but there was never any chemistry so I gave up. Don't misunderstand, I've been very happy with my situation and I don't feel lonely. I have friends and family, and my connections with my Reiki clients, so I'm not exactly a hermit." Annalise stopped, aware that she might be protesting more than she needed to be.

"I know what you mean. I married later in life because I wasn't willing to lose my independence and didn't buy into that belief of thinking I needed a husband to fulfill me despite what our generation had been led to believe. Then when I did get married, it didn't work. I'd become too set in my ways and didn't think I'd ever be in a relationship again, but then I met Jim. We have a great relationship even though we live apart and don't have any marriage plans in our future. We spend time together, but have our own lives, too, so it's the best of both worlds."

"I can relate to that. I just never met my Jim," Annalise said.

"Until now?"

"There's definitely an attraction and a spark that I haven't felt since Peter."

"From the way he was looking at you, I think the feeling was mutual," Eva said, grinning.

"It did look like that, didn't it?" Annalise said, returning her smile.

I smell fish! Eva's cat, Reuben said as he trotted into the dining room.

"Well, hello, Reuben. I'm surprised it took you this long to pester me," Eva told him, using her animal whisperer skills to communicate with him.

I was sleeping, he defended himself. *And I'm not pestering. You were gone all morning and my bowl is empty, if you'd cared enough to check.*

"I hardly think you're going to starve to death, but I'll share *some* of my fish with you," she said, walking to the kitchen to put some in his bowl.

Annalise looked on with amusement. Although she didn't have Eva's powers to understand the other side of her conversation, she was able to get the gist. And Annalise could have sworn that he'd blinked a knowing wink at her before he followed along behind Eva. She crumpled up the wrapper for the veggie sandwich she'd been eating and joined them in the kitchen to toss it in the garbage.

"I'm going to head home. I think I need a nap after the day we've put in and it was an early start," she said.

"That's not a bad idea. I may do the same," Eva said, yawning.

"I'll see you tomorrow! And you be good for your mom," Annalise told Reuben who was giving his face an after-lunch wash with his paws. He looked up at her with disdain, one paw in midair and a bit of his tongue sticking out, making Annalise laugh. "No need to translate that, Eva. Talk to you later!"

The sound of a phone ringing pulled Annalise out of a dream. *She was in the cafeteria standing behind their table with the others. Shoppers were milling around the other vendors' tables. She felt her attention drawn to one in particular at the far end of the room. Their back was to her, but when they turned to face her, they were wearing a mask.*

She rubbed her eyes and reached for the phone on her nightstand. She was tempted to ignore it and go back to sleep, but it was her business line. After saying hello, a deep, male voice answered on the other end of the line.

"Annalise? It's Liam Campbell. I hope you don't mind that I got your phone number from Bethany Cox."

Annalise bolted up and was suddenly wide awake. Her stomach erupted with a swarm of butterflies.

"Liam. How nice to hear from you and, of course, it's not a problem." Inwardly, she was debating whether she should thank or curse Bethany for giving him her number.

"I was wondering if you might be free for dinner tonight? I wanted to ask you earlier but I had to be at my table the entire time. And then with all the confusion going on after Willow's allergic reaction, I didn't get the chance. You'd already left by the time I got my things packed."

"Oh," her brain scrambled to find words.

"Unless you've already made plans. I realize I'm not giving you much time," he said, his voice registering disappointment.

"No, no, it's not that," she said quickly. "I'm just surprised. I wasn't expecting it. But, yes, I'd love to go to dinner with you. Tell me when and where and I'll meet you at the restaurant."

"How about six o'clock at Twenty-five Park Circle?"

"That will work. I've been wanting to try it out ever since they opened last month. I'll see you there."

They disconnected the call but she remained in her bed with the phone cradled against her chest. She felt a twinge of guilt as though she was cheating on Peter, despite the fact that it had been three decades since he died in a motorcycle accident, four years after they were married.

You've dated other men. What's your hangup about this one?

Because he's different. You have chemistry with this one, the voice in her head answered.

She glanced at the clock on her nightstand. If she was going to be on time, she'd need to get ready now. The meditation she'd planned to do would have to wait.

CHAPTER 6

"As everyone ready for today?" Jennifer asked. She had Boscoe with her again. "He was a customer magnet yesterday so I brought Boscoe with me," she explained.

"That's fine with me. You're a good boy, aren't you, Boscoe?" Eva said rhetorically, giving him a belly rub when he rolled over and looked at her as though expecting that result. When she stopped, he rolled over again and jumped to his feet.

Thanks, Eva, that felt terrific.

"You're most welcome, Boscoe."

By now, they had their set-up routine down to a science and before long, their table was ready for business. Eva looked over and caught Annalise stealing a glance at Liam who was still putting out his pottery.

"I think I'll go ask Liam if he needs any help while we're waiting for the doors to open," Annalise said. She gave Eva a pointed glare, daring her to make a comment but she only raised her eyebrows.

"That's fine with me," Sarah answered.

"Me, too," Jennifer said.

"I think we can handle things until then," Eva said, giving Annalise a Cheshire cat grin.

"Is it just me, or does Annalise have a glow about her today?" Jennifer asked when Annalise had gone out of earshot.

Sarah looked over to Liam's table where he and Annalise were putting out his pottery display, and laughing as though they were sharing a private joke. "Now that you mention it, I think you're right. Sure looks like she and Liam have hit it off."

"I see it, too, Jen. Good for her," Eva said.

They gave each other a knowing smile and sat in their seats to rest until the day's rush of customers began. As if on cue, Bethany announced the doors would open in five minutes. Annalise returned in time to be at their table, her face flushed.

"I didn't say anything," Eva said under her breath.

"Thanks," Annalise whispered with her head down, focused on rearranging the display of table runners in front of her. When she glanced up, Liam was looking directly at her and gave her a wink before turning to greet the customer at his table.

"Oh, you two have got it so bad," Sarah said to Annalise, a grin on her face from ear to ear.

Annalise was rescued from any more comments by the arrival of a group of women. The next ninety minutes passed quickly with eager customers stopping at their table to find gifts for their holiday list. A loud commotion at Sophia Peterson's table caught everyone's attention and all eyes turned to her as the room suddenly got quiet enough to hear the proverbial pin drop. A group of four women were gathered around one of her paintings and Benjamin Brooks was standing off to the side with his camera poised to take a picture.

"Somebody slashed my painting!" Sophia was directing her anger at Bethany Cox. "It was fine when I brought it in and set it up, so it had to have happened here. I was about to sell it to this lady when she noticed the tear. Now it's ruined!"

Annalise felt her arms prickle with the tingling sensation that happened when her intuition sensed something more was going on.

"Has Miles Clarke been here today?" Sophia demanded to know.

"I... I think I saw him earlier," Bethany replied, taken aback by the forcefulness of Sophia's question.

"I bet he did it when I had my back turned. He's always been jealous of my work. If you don't ask him, then I will. And I might do it through the police!" Sophia threatened.

"Now settle down, Sophia," Violet intervened in a calming tone. "Are you sure you didn't accidentally snag it on something when you were setting it up? Maybe there's a sharp edge on your easel. Let's check it now before we get the police involved."

Sophia didn't look convinced but Violet was already behind the table and picked up the painting. She ran her finger over the wood frame in the spot where the painting had rested. "Ow!" She pulled her finger away and a small spot of blood was oozing out. She held it up for Sophia and everyone else to see. "I think we've found your slasher."

"Oh," Sophia's anger deflated. "That must be how it happened." Her words came out in a subdued tone of voice as she took the painting from Violet and put it in the empty tote under her table. She folded up the easel and placed it under the table as well.

Sensing the drama was over, the chatter of voices began once again and the groups of people scattered around the room observing the scene dispersed.

"Well, that was interesting," Eva commented.

"I'll say!" Jennifer agreed.

"Do things usually get that heated in Glen Lake?" Sarah asked.

"Not that I know of. I didn't realize Sophia and Miles were rivals. He's a painter, too," Jennifer explained for Sarah's benefit.

Annalise remained quiet and was still focused on Sophia, filing away what she'd seen to think about later. Benjamin had remained off to the side as the scene had unfolded and Annalise observed him taking several pictures documenting the confrontation. *Looks like Mr. Brooks isn't interested in only the feel-good aspects of rural craft artisans. I wonder if this kind of thing happens in other places, too,* she thought.

"Time to wrap it up," Eva announced an hour later. The shoppers were mostly gone with only a few stragglers still shopping, but Bethany was letting them know that the fair was winding down and it was time to go.

"That was fun but I'm glad it's over and we only have one more weekend," Jennifer said.

"Me, too. I'm looking forward to some quality time with my couch. These folding chairs are like sitting on rocks!" Sarah said.

Eva chuckled. "I have to agree. Even with all the extra cushioning on my back side, they were a little hard for my comfort."

"Maybe we should bring in some seat cushions next week," Annalise suggested.

"Great idea! I have some I can bring for us," Jennifer offered.

"Works for me. I don't think we have anything like that at home," Sarah said.

"Okay, Boscoe. It's time for us to go home now," Jennifer said, unhooking him from the leg of her chair. He jumped up on all fours and then hopped on his hind legs to do a little dance. "It's been a long day for you, too, hasn't it, buddy?" He let out a single *woof* which Eva didn't have to translate for them to understand.

The four women shambled out of the cafeteria dragging their totes behind them in sharp contrast to the energetic way they'd arrived. No one spoke until they reached their cars and then it was only to say goodbye. Annalise was the last to pull out of her parking spot, but as she put the car in gear she spotted Liam waving at her. Her pulse quickened and she felt a burst of energy reviving her when he walked toward her. She had put the window down and knew she had a silly grin on her face by the time he leaned down to speak, but wasn't able to stop herself.

"I don't know about you, but I'm too tired to cook tonight. Would it be too soon for you to have dinner with me again?"

Pull yourself together, Annalise, and wipe that grin off your face! She pressed her lips together and composed her face in what she hoped was a more dignified expression. "No, it's not too soon. I was thinking about whether I have any meals in my freezer I could microwave, so you don't have to twist my arm."

"Any suggestions?"

"Yes. I suggest we stay away from The Checkout. I'm not ready for Betty Jones to speculate about whether we're a couple."

He guffawed at the remark about Betty, the server at Glen Lake's only restaurant and resident town crier. "She wouldn't only speculate. She'd have half the town in on it by the end of the week."

"You're not giving her enough credit. I'd give it two days," Annalise retorted. "How about The Pines restaurant in an hour? Would that give you enough time to take your pottery back to your house first?"

"Plenty of time. I'll meet you there." He smiled and held her gaze for a moment before walking back to his car.

She put her car in Drive and pulled out of the parking lot, her plans to meditate on the incidents of the past two weekends fading into the background.

CHAPTER 7

After dinner, they had met at Annalise's house and talked for hours. It was only when she couldn't control a huge yawn that he suggested reluctantly that he should leave. *You've got a client coming in at ten, Annalise. You're going to need to get some rest*, her better judgement stepped in to stop her from disagreeing so that he would stay longer.

She fell asleep almost as soon as her head hit the pillow.

———

There was a knock on the door and a voice announced, "Room Service." When no one replied, the door opened and a woman entered the room pushing a rolling cart on which there were two metal domed dishes, eating utensils, a carafe, and beverage glasses. She rolled the cart to the small, round table and two chairs near the windows and turned to leave the room. As she did, her eyes were drawn to the floor beside the bed. At first her mind was confused by the sight of a man, motionless, crumpled on the floor. It took only a nano-second before it registered that the man was dead. She gasped and covered her mouth to hold back a scream.

She ran from the room not bothering to close the door behind her.

Five minutes later a man in a suit arrived. His mouth was pursed and he was frowning as he walked briskly across the room. The room service delivery woman hovered in the hallway. The guy's probably just passed out drunk had been his first thought when the server had found him and said there was a dead man in Room 214. When he got closer to the bed, though, it was obvious that she'd been telling the truth. He didn't want to, but he knew he would have to check to be sure, and felt the man's throat for a pulse. There was none. He willed himself to walk, not run, from the room. Before closing the door, he took the Do Not Disturb placard from the door handle and placed it onto the side of the handle facing the hallway.

"Make sure no one goes in there. I'm going to call 911."

She nodded her head several times, too frightened to speak.

The next sound was that of a siren announcing the arrival of an ambulance pulling into the hotel parking lot. The manager opened the door and two paramedics entered the room with their trauma kit.

"I'd say he's been dead for hours," one of them said.

The other EMT nodded. "That's what I'd say, too."

Another siren sounded in the parking lot and not long after, a policeman entered the room.

"Who besides the EMTs have been in the room?" he asked the manager.

"Only room service and me, but only as far as the bed. He looked to the server and she nodded to confirm what he'd said. I immediately locked the room and no one has been in until the EMTs arrived."

"We'll take it from here. Where can we find you when we need more information?"

The hotel manager pulled a business card out of his inside coat pocket and handed it to the policeman and turned to leave.

"Wait. What's his name?"

"It's Benjamin Brooks."

———

Annalise's eyes fluttered open. The thin morning light of early December barely illuminated the room. She shivered, in part from the temperature of the room, but also from the afterimages of her dream still in her mind and the voice in her head telling her:

It wasn't an accident. He was murdered.

CHAPTER 8

Annalise turned off silent mode on her phone once her client's session was over and heard the ping of a voice mail notification.

She listened to Eva's animated voice telling her *You need to call me as soon as you get this message!* and knew immediately why she would be calling. She made herself a cup of tea first and took it to her bedroom sitting room, her favorite spot in her house. She took her phone out of her pocket but changed her mind about returning Eva's call and placed it on the table beside her chair instead. She rested her feet on the ottoman and sipped the tea as she looked out the second story window at the landscape below. The grass was brown now instead of the vivid green of summer and the trees at the far edge of the property which bordered the river were a mixture of evergreens and naked branches barren of their leaves. Despite its starkness, the familiar scenery calmed her and within minutes it was enough for her to feel centered. She picked up her phone from the table beside her chair and pushed the button for Eva's number.

Eva launched into her news as soon as she answered the call. "You're never going to believe what I heard at The Checkout!"

"Benjamin Brooks is dead," Annalise interrupted.

"How did… ? Ohh, you had a vision, didn't you?" Eva's voice sounded deflated as she answered her own question.

"Well, a dream, but yes. What did you hear about it?" Annalise wanted to find out what the gossip mill had to say before telling Eva Benjamin wasn't just dead, he'd been murdered.

"Jim and I were at The Checkout for breakfast. Bethany Cox had told Betty about it. They found him dead in his hotel room last night. She was supposed to meet him this morning but had to cancel. When she called, he didn't answer his phone, so she called the hotel and asked to be put through to his room. I'm sure the clerk wasn't supposed to say so, but he told her Benjamin had had an accident and was dead."

"It wasn't an accident. It was murder."

"Are you sure?" Eva asked.

"I am. I'm not always certain when I have dreams like this, but I have no doubt about this one being true. Did she know if they've already declared it an accident or are they investigating the possibility of it being a murder?"

"If they are, she either didn't know or didn't say. Do you think Phil or Dennis would tell us?"

"In my dream I only saw his body face down on the floor and there was no obvious sign it was a murder. If they think it was accidental, they wouldn't have assigned it to Homicide."

"Should we tell them anyway? They have a history with us after being part of five of their murder investigations. I think they'd believe you," Eva said.

"It would have been easier if they are already aware of his death, but you're right that I should talk to them. If they dismiss it as an accident, the murderer will literally get away with murder."

"Do you know who it is?"

"No, but I think it's connected to the craft fair somehow. I still haven't had anything conclusive jumping out at me, but I could sense an undercurrent of negative energy both weekends we've been there."

"Do you think we should talk to the other vendors? One of them might know something without even being aware of it," Eva suggested.

"That's a good idea, Eva. We'll have to wait, though. It would sound suspicious if we started asking questions before it's actually been declared a murder."

"Oh, right. Will you still call Phil or Dennis sooner, though?"

"I think I'm going to give it another day or two. They will probably have to do an autopsy because of the circumstances and it will take them that long to get any results. They would be more likely to give more credence to my dream if the autopsy shows it wasn't an accident." She glanced at the clock on her table. "I'm going to have to talk to you later, Eva. I have a client coming in a half hour and I need to get ready for that."

They disconnected the call, but Annalise remained where she was. Her thoughts kept returning to the scene in her dream. *You don't have time to think about this now.* Her inner voice's warning finally convinced her to take her cup to the kitchen and ready herself for the client as she'd told Eva she needed to do. For now, she'd have to compartmentalize her thoughts and focus on her client.

CHAPTER 9

She had another dream-filled night. This time, her point of view was focused on the luggage stand where Benjamin's suitcase was lying. Beside it was a camera bag. Annalise reached into the bag and pulled out the camera. She felt a nudge to open the slot for the memory card and found it empty.

That's it! she thought upon waking. The killer wanted to keep his photos from becoming public. *But what about the photos was so dangerous that they were willing to kill Benjamin for them?* She closed her eyes hoping to hook into the dream again, but the connection had been broken and the answer to that question wasn't forthcoming.

Benjamin's death hadn't been reported either in the newspaper or on any of the TV stations the day before, leading her to believe that the authorities still hadn't made a decision about his cause of death. *If I tell the detectives it was a murder and they should investigate, I could ruin their trust in us.* It was that possibility that was holding her back from contacting them. She tossed back the covers and put on her slippers. As she was walking toward the kitchen for her morning coffee, another thought came to her. *They know me and what I can do. I can tell them I've had these dreams and let them decide if they want to follow up. The ladies and I can still talk to the vendors on Saturday and if we find out anything more, we can tell them that, too. If I don't, and this really is murder, there would be a killer on the loose in the area and I could be responsible if they kill again.* She stood with the coffee scoop in mid-air, startled by that idea. *Don't be dramatic, Annalise, this isn't about a serial killer.* She was reassured by that thought and the sensation of knowing it was true. As she went about her daily routine, though, her thoughts kept coming back to the voice in her head telling her she should call the detectives.

"*Alright!* I'll call them," she said aloud to make it stop.

Her first appointment wasn't until after lunch so she had no excuse not to do it now. She retrieved her phone from its charging station and scrolled through her contacts. She wavered with her finger poised over their numbers but a final nudge of her conscience urged her on to make the call.

"Detective Roberts."

"Phil, this is Annalise Jordan. After all this time, I'm not sure if I have to say this, but I hope you can listen to what I have to say with an open mind." She cringed when she heard her nervous laughter. *So much for trying to sound confident, Annalise.*

"O-*kay*," he replied hesitantly.

She took a deep breath and began. After telling him about her first dream and her belief that Benjamin Brooks had been murdered, there was silence on the line. *Uh oh. You were right to worry. He thinks you're nuts and you've blown it.*

"If it wasn't for the fact that we've worked together, this would be the part where I would thank you for your call and hang up. Dennis and I were just assigned this case fifteen minutes before you called."

"He was lying face down when you found him and it wasn't obvious at first it was murder," Annalise said.

"Yes, that's right."

"Did you examine his camera?"

"His camera?"

"Yes, in the dream I had this morning it was in the camera bag beside his suitcase on the luggage rack. The memory card was missing and I believe the killer took it. I think whatever was on that memory card is the reason Benjamin was killed," Annalise said.

She heard the sound of papers shuffling in the background.

"Here it is," Phil said. "The inventory of what was in his room includes a camera, and you're right. It was found right where you said it was."

Despite her conviction that she'd been right, Annalise was relieved to have it validated.

"Do you have any ideas about who the killer is?" Phil asked.

"No, I don't. Except that I think it's connected to the craft fair in Glen Lake. You may already be aware that was his reason for being in the area. On the surface, there's nothing about it that makes it obvious, but there have been some incidents that I think are connected. Eva and I have talked about speaking with the other vendors to see if we could find out more. We'll be at the fair on Saturday and Sunday, along with Jennifer and Sarah. It's the last weekend for the craft fair. We'd be happy to do that and let you know what we find out," she offered.

Once again, there was silence on the other end of the line as the detective considered.

"I hope I don't lose my job because of this, but sure, ask around to see what you can find out. They might be more willing to talk to you. If you find out something we should know, call me. On second thought, even if you don't, give me their names by Monday and we'll follow up anyway."

"We can do that. I promise."

"Please don't make me regret this," he said.

————

Eva answered on the second ring.

"I couldn't call you until now because I had clients, but I

spoke with Phil Roberts this morning. I told him about my dreams…"

"Dreams?" Eva interrupted. "You had another one?"

"Oh, right. You didn't know about that either." She told Eva about her dream and her intuition that the killer took the memory card because it could incriminate them.

"Phil wasn't completely on board at first, but then he agreed it might be helpful for us to talk to the vendors this weekend. His thinking was that they might be more willing to talk to us and not withhold information. He asked me to let him know what, if anything, we learned."

"It might not be easy to do that if it's anything like the past two weekends, but we can try."

"It actually might be less conspicuous if we split up and find a moment when they're less busy. We can make it look like we're doing some shopping for ourselves," Annalise suggested.

"That's a possibility. We'll have to play it by ear. In the meantime, we can both be thinking about a Plan B."

"And maybe a Plan C, but I'm convinced this is connected to the vendors even if they aren't aware of it. The problem is going to be not tipping off the killer by asking the wrong questions of the wrong person."

CHAPTER 10

Annalise and Eva agreed to meet at the craft fair earlier than usual on Saturday hoping to set up their items and have time before it started to talk to vendors. Not everyone else had the same idea, though, so they had to wait for the others to show up. One of the first to arrive was Liam. They had spoken during the week but Annalise's stomach turned to butterflies as soon as she spotted him. He caught her looking and shot her a smile, making the butterflies dance even more.

"Why don't you go give him a hand setting up and while you're at it, you can ask him if he's seen anything suspicious?" Eva said, making Annalise jump. Her attention had been entirely focused on Liam and she didn't realize Eva had been observing the interaction between the two of them.

Annalise turned to Eva who was giving her another Cheshire cat grin. "You saw that, huh?"

"Only a blind person could have missed it," Eva teased. "Seriously, though, go ahead. He might have seen something we missed. Vanessa Barnes is coming in now. I'll offer to help her and maybe she'll have some information that will be helpful." She rose to greet Vanessa, leaving Annalise to compose herself before speaking to Liam.

"Good morning, Vanessa. Can I help carry anything in for you? Annalise and I got here early, so I'm just sitting here twiddling my thumbs," Eva said.

"What?" Vanessa said, distractedly, her hands full. "Oh, thank you. I could use some help bringing in my stuff if you don't mind." She gave Eva an appreciative smile.

"Glad to help my neighbor," Eva told her. "I'll follow you out."

Vanessa put the small totes she'd brought in under her table and they walked out to her car.

"It's been quite an eventful week, hasn't it? You've heard about Benjamin Brooks?" Eva asked.

"Yes! The news report says they're calling it a murder," Vanessa looked up from the tote she was handing to Eva, her eyes were round with surprise.

"I heard that, too. I can't imagine who would have wanted to kill him," Eva said.

"Well, this is probably nothing," Vanessa said, lowering her voice. "But last weekend I was taking a bathroom break and Benjamin and Bethany were arguing in the lobby. It looked pretty heated and I'm sure I heard Bethany tell him *she wouldn't let him get away with it*." Vanessa said, raising her eyebrows and nodding her head as she put dramatic emphasis on the words and then paused to let it sink in.

"Get away with what?" Eva asked, adding her own touch of drama to her voice. *This could be a good lead*, she thought, but kept her expression neutral.

"I don't know. As soon as they realized I was there, they stopped arguing. Bethany told him the conversation wasn't over, but she'd see him later and they both walked away."

They had reached the cafeteria and Bethany was walking toward them, ending their conversation.

"Is there anything else you need help with, ladies?"

"No, but thank you. I'm glad we only have one more day to do this. It sounded like a great idea when I signed up, but the thrill wore off last week."

Eva chuckled. "We know exactly what you mean, Vanessa. If you don't mind some unsolicited feedback, Bethany, that would be the first thing on my list. If you do this again next year, I think one weekend would be plenty."

"Duly noted. It's not the first time I've heard that, so you may be onto something." Bethany's smile was genuine. "I have to go, but perhaps we can talk more later. Abigail is trying to get my attention." She smiled her farewell before walking toward Abigail's table.

"Oh, look, Jennifer brought Boscoe again!"

Eva followed Vanessa's eyes and saw Jennifer with Boscoe on his leash in one hand and her rolling tote in the other. "Let me give you a hand," she said, walking over to Jennifer and holding out her hand for Boscoe's leash. He looked up at her with a doggie grin as she leaned over to scratch his head.

Thank you, Eva. That feels great!

"Good morning, Boscoe. Are you ready for another day at the fair?"

Anyone listening would have thought this a typical rhetorical conversation between a dog and a human even when Boscoe responded with a *woof!*

It's been fun to meet everyone and get all the attention, but I'd be happy to be at home, too.

"I know just what you mean, buddy," she said, bending down to attach his leash to Jennifer's chair. She gave him one last chin scratch before helping Jennifer set up the decorations on their table.

"I'm sorry I'm late," Sarah said, rushing in.

"You're not late," Jennifer said, giving her a reassuring smile. "I just got here myself a couple minutes ago. We've still got a few minutes before they open the doors for customers."

"I overslept this morning. I never oversleep, but doesn't it figure, today would be the day?"

Eva patted her arm. "It's okay, Sarah, really. We've got this routine down now and it won't take us any time at all to set up. Jennifer and I can do the decorating while you get your things put out."

"Where's Annalise?" Sarah asked, noticing she wasn't the last of the four to arrive at the table.

"She's at Liam's table helping him set up," Eva said, with a smirk. "Oh, wait, here she comes now."

Sarah turned to see Annalise walking toward them, a scowl on her face as she looked in Eva's direction.

"You can wipe that smirk off your face," Annalise said to Eva, trying, but not succeeding, to sound annoyed.

Eva swiped her hand across her mouth to reveal a sober expression.

"What am I missing?" Sarah whispered to Jennifer, who was trying to hide a smile of her own.

"Eva's teasing Annalise about having something going on with Liam," Jennifer whispered back, but kept her eyes averted from Annalise.

"Ohhh," Sarah replied, and looked toward Liam's table. He was looking in Annalise's direction, his eyes soft and a slight smile on his face. "I'd say you're right."

CHAPTER 11

"That wraps up another successful day," Eva declared when the last of the customers had filed out of the cafeteria. "Jim and I are going to The Checkout for an early dinner. I almost told him he could go by himself. He tried to rub it in about my having to be here until the fair is over and that he could leave early and relax at home since they decided to shorten the hours for the Santa booth today. But then I realized turning down his invitation would mean having to cook. Would you like to join us?"

"I wish I could, but I need to take Boscoe home and I promised Dave and the kids we could have pizza tonight. Rain check?"

"Absolutely!"

"I can come. Ashley has a work thing so I was going to order takeout, anyway," Sarah said.

Annalise paused packing the last of her things, looking toward Liam, as if deciding whether to join the ladies. She nodded her head, decision made, and put the last stocking into her tote before snapping on its lid. "Sure, but would you mind if I asked Liam, too?"

No more jabs, Eva. What are you, twelve? I think Annalise is serious about this guy, she thought. "Of course not. Jim would probably welcome having another man in the group."

"I'm done packing up, so I'll go ask him now."

Annalise returned a moment later. "He said he'd be happy to join us. He'll meet us there once he gets packed. I offered to help him so it wouldn't take so long."

"Sounds like a plan. I think I'm ready to go, so I'll call Jim now and he can save us a table. I think a booth would be too crowded," Eva said. "Will you be bringing Boscoe again tomorrow, Jen?"

"I think so. Would you ask him if that's okay with him?"

Woof! Woof! Boscoe replied, even before Eva had a chance to ask.

"He says he'd like to come, especially since it's the last day," Eva translated.

"In that case, we'll both see you tomorrow." Jennifer unhooked his leash from her chair and waved goodbye, rolling her cart behind her.

Annalise followed, stopping at Liam's spot. She took a sheet of paper from the stack he'd placed on his table and wrapped it around a mug before placing it in the box behind his table.

"I'm all packed, too," Sarah said. "I'm glad I didn't bring everything I had in my inventory. I don't think I would have had much to sell tomorrow if I hadn't."

"That was smart thinking. Should we go?" Eva asked.

"Let's do it!"

Jim's car was in the parking lot of The Checkout Diner when they each arrived in their own cars. The aroma of burgers, fries, coffee, hot chocolate, and peppermint wafted toward them when they opened the door.

"Over here," Jim called out, waving to catch Eva's attention.

"I almost didn't recognize you out of uniform," Sarah said, smiling.

A puzzled look came over Jim's face until he realized she was talking about his Santa suit, not his police uniform. "Now I get it. I was wondering when you would have seen me in my trooper's uniform. I didn't ever stop you for a ticket, did I?" he joked.

"No, but I haven't sat on Santa's lap recently either," she teased back.

Betty Jones, Checkout's server and gossip extraordinaire, bustled over to their table, menus in hand.

"Did Jim tell you we've got two more coming?" Eva asked. "They should be here soon, but I think we'll wait to put our food orders in. I could kill for a cup of coffee, though."

"I'll have a glass of water with lemon, please," Sarah said.

"I'll have another cup of coffee," Jim said. When Eva gave him a disapproving look, he responded with a smile. "Don't worry, it's decaf."

Jim glanced toward the door and waved to catch Annalise's attention. "Annalise just came in, and that must be Liam with her."

"Jim, this is Liam Campbell. Liam, Jim Davis," Annalise introduced them as they took their seats.

"You look familiar. Have we met?" Liam asked.

"I don't think so, but it might be because you've seen me in my Santa disguise at the craft fair."

Liam's face brightened as he got the connection. "Yes! I think that's got to be it. It's all about the eyes."

Betty returned with two place settings and menus. "I'll give you a few minutes to look over the menus," she said after taking their drink orders. "The specials are on the board if you want to order off the menu."

"I think I've decided. Everybody else ready to order?" Jim asked after they'd had time to choose and motioned to Betty they were ready when everyone nodded.

"Have you been having a good time at the craft fair?" he asked Liam.

"It wasn't exactly what I'd expected. I'm not sure what that was, but, yeah, I think I have been having a good time. It got me out into the community and I've met some very nice people," he said and looked over at Annalise, who blushed.

Jim's eyebrows raised slightly as he looked at Eva, and she shook her head only enough for him to notice. He understood that was an *I'll tell you later* response.

"What brings all of you in today?" Betty asked, order pad in hand.

"We've been at the craft fair. We've been selling, not buying," Eva replied.

Betty's eyes lit up, and those who knew her weren't surprised when she began her next remarks with a bit of gossip.

"Everyone's been talking about that Benjamin Brooks thing. Quentin Gray didn't have much nice to say about him. I didn't get all the details, but apparently he took an unflattering picture of Quentin's woodworking that ended up in a bad review about ten or eleven years ago and it nearly cost Quentin his business. That's why he moved away from where he'd been living to start over here. It took him a long time to build back his reputation and get his business back on track. He was pretty upset when he found out that Benjamin was here to take photos for a new book. He was worried that the same thing might happen again and he told Bethany he didn't want his picture taken."

"That's very interesting. I didn't pick up on that at all, but it's been pretty busy every weekend so I wasn't paying a lot of attention to whom Benjamin was photographing," Eva said.

"Quentin doesn't strike me as the type to be violent, though. I can't imagine he'd have anything to do with what happened to Mr. Brooks. Have you all decided what you want to order?" Betty moved from the one thought to the other without a beat between, putting an end to the topic of whether Quentin Gray had a motive for the murder.

"What do you think about that, Annalise?" Eva asked once Betty left to give the orders to the diner's cook, Sam. She carefully avoided making any reference to her question being directed at Annalise because of her psychic abilities.

"On the surface, I can't imagine Quentin being that motivated to kill Benjamin, either. People can do some unexpected things when pushed, though. I'd have to think about it some more. If I come up with anything, I'll let you know."

"You're right about that, Annalise. I was involved in some cases when I was a trooper that defied explanation as to why something would have set someone off to the point they'd commit murder," Jim agreed.

"How many years were you with the police?" Liam asked.

"About forty years. I joined the Maine State Police right out of college."

"Wow, that's a long time. You must have experienced a lot."

"I did, but how about you? How long have you been a potter? Is that the right word? It doesn't sound right when I say it out loud," Jim asked.

Liam smiled. "Potter is the right word. It started out as a hobby when I was in college. I was majoring in art and thought I'd become an art teacher. That was so I could make a living until I could get my paintings into galleries and actually make a living at it. I took a pottery class and that changed the entire direction of my career path. I fell in love with the medium. I still do some painting, but it's pottery that is my passion."

"Did you have to teach for a while anyway?" Eva asked. "I'm a retired schoolteacher myself."

"Oh! No offense meant about only wanting to do it until I could move on," Liam said.

"No offense taken," Eva said, smiling. "You wouldn't be the first or last to say that."

"To answer your question, yes, I did teach, and did the pottery on the side. I slowly built up a clientele of gift shops on the coast. It took me about five years, but I've been able to make a living at it since then. I still teach a class now and then but they're mostly workshops, not full-time."

"Your pieces are amazing. Even the practical ones like the mugs and bowls are so unique. They're pieces of artwork,"

Annalise said, groaning inwardly as soon as the words were out of her mouth. *Oh, for the love of Pete, Annalise. You sound like you're gushing.*

"You're too kind."

Liam's reaction didn't help curb her embarrassment even though she knew he wasn't trying to make fun of her, but she couldn't take the words back now. The group fell silent and as soon as it began to be awkward, Liam picked up the conversation. "How about you, Sarah? You haven't said what you do for your day job."

"I work from home for a cyber-security firm. It isn't the most exciting job most days, but being part of the Cozy Quilts Club has helped feed my creative side. These ladies have become more than just friends, they're like sisters to me."

"Aww, aren't you sweet, Sarah? You know, I feel the same way," Eva said.

Betty appeared with a row of three plates stacked along her left arm and two in her right hand, to the amazement of everyone at the table. She deftly set the plates down in front of each of them as though it wasn't a big deal.

"Does anyone need a refill on their drinks?" When no one asked for one, she left them with an "enjoy your meal," and hurried to the door to greet the next set of patrons arriving.

I get what Annalise sees in him, Eva was thinking by the end of their meal. He fit into the group as if he'd been a part of it from the beginning and she noticed that even Jim was chatting with him as if they were old buddies.

Sarah's phone dinged. "It's Ashley wondering when I'll be home," she explained. "I've been having such a good time, I didn't realize how late it was. I'd better go, but I'll see you all tomorrow."

"Reuben is going to be very annoyed with me. I had no idea it was this late!" Eva said, picking up her tab and rising to leave.

"I'll follow you home if you're up for a visit," Jim suggested.

"I don't need to make any more stuff for the craft fair, so my evening is wide open," Eva said.

I want to invite him to come home with me but maybe I should wait until we get outside. He might not want people to know we're dating. *Is that even what this is?* Annalise was thinking, when Liam came to the rescue.

"I could use some company tonight, too. Are you available, Annalise?"

Her shoulders relaxed and she smiled from ear to ear. "I am."

CHAPTER 12

Eva and Annalise arrived at the craft fair at the same time on the final Sunday.

"That was a lot of fun yesterday. Jim couldn't stop talking about what a great guy Liam is. I was beginning to feel a little jealous," Eva said facetiously as they walked companionably into the cafeteria, making Annalise laugh.

"It was nice. I was worried about whether Liam might feel like I was rushing things with our relationship. We talked about it last night and decided that's what this is…a relationship. Never thought I'd be saying that again. We're going to see where it goes."

"I couldn't be happier for you, Annalise. I don't think you *need* someone to complete you. But after Jim and I dated for a while, I realized I liked having someone in my life to go places with and be a companion. After being a teacher for so many years… well, decades… I began to miss some of that human interaction once I'd been retired for a while. Reuben has his moments, but it wasn't enough. Don't get me wrong, I still need my personal space."

"I understand what you're saying. The Quilt Club and my clients have filled some of that hole for me, but the past couple of weeks made me realize that thinking I'd shut the door permanently on a romantic relationship could be open to change."

"Or it could be that what you needed was for the right person to come along," Eva said. "Speaking of..." She stopped before finishing the sentence when Liam looked in their direction and walked toward them.

"What can I help you ladies with today?"

"We're traveling light today. I'm all set. How about you, Eva?"

"I'm all set, but thanks for the offer. I was telling Annalise that I'm a little jealous of you."

Liam tilted his head slightly and his eyebrows scrunched together. "Excuse me?"

Eva began to laugh. "Just teasing. Jim was quite taken with you. You may be his new bestie."

"Ohh," Liam said, smiling broadly. "I enjoyed his company, too. I hope we'll be seeing more of each other after the fair is over."

"I think you can count on that."

Annalise hung back to talk to Liam as Eva continued walking toward their table. Missing this morning were the volunteers setting up the Santa display because the school had given them permission to leave it in place overnight. *Something is different about the vibe in the room*, Eva sensed. It wasn't just the physical surroundings. The air itself had a sense of foreboding. *I'm not even psychic and I'm aware of it. I wonder what Annalise thinks.*

Annalise pulled her tote to her spot beside Eva and began placing the last of her wares on the table. She looked up and glanced around the room.

"Something feels off," she said, as much to herself as Eva.

"I feel it, too."

"I don't know what it is about this space, but I can't tune into its energies. Whenever I try to penetrate what's underneath, it's like I'm walking into a brick wall of negativity," Annalise said, leveling her eyes with Eva's.

They heard a soft woof, and turned to see Jennifer, Boscoe, and Sarah walking in.

"Last weekend I felt like this was going on forever, but now that it's the last day, it seems like it's flown by," Jennifer said.

"That's how I feel, too. Ashley couldn't believe it either when I was leaving and told her it's the last day," Sarah said.

Eva took the leash from Jennifer and repeated her greeting ritual with Boscoe, talking softly to him with her back to the room in case anyone was watching.

Bethany clapped her hands to get everyone's attention. "I'm opening the doors now. Have a great last day and thank you to everyone. I think it's been a success and I hope we can do it again next year!" There were a few low groans from some of the vendor tables, but Bethany either didn't hear or ignored them.

"Even Santa has lost his zippity do dah," Eva chuckled, as Jim shuffled to his place.

"I think there's even more people here than we had last week," Sarah commented when they had their first break of people visiting their table.

"I think they know it's their last chance to buy something from us so there might be a little FOMO going on," Jennifer said. "Speaking of last chances, I should take Boscoe out for a walk. I heard him whimpering when that last group stopped here."

"Go right ahead. We can cover for you if anyone comes while you're gone," Annalise offered.

Jennifer unhooked Boscoe from the chair and walked toward the entrance, pulling on her gloves as they walked, when she felt a tug on the leash. Looking back, she saw Boscoe nosing through a box under Quentin Gray's table. She pulled gently on the leash but he continued snuffling through the box and whining softly. Quentin was distracted with customers and didn't notice. *I better go over and find out what he's after,* she thought. As soon as she walked back to Boscoe, he looked up at Jennifer and she could see something in his mouth. *Don't swallow that!* she thought, panicked.

"Drop it," she said in a whisper, bending down to his level and holding out her hand to catch whatever it was. As soon as it landed in her hand, images filled her head. A brown leather-gloved hand was holding a camera and removing the memory card with their other hand. Jennifer knew instantly it was what she now had in her hand. And, that it belonged to Benjamin Brooks.

CHAPTER 13

She dropped the card back into the box, grateful that she'd put her gloves on before touching it. She stood, looking around to see if anyone had seen her, but everyone's attention was elsewhere.

"Come on, Boscoe, let's take you for a walk but it will have to be a short one. I need to go back to tell the ladies about this."

"Are you okay, Jen?" Sarah asked when Jennifer returned to their table.

Annalise and Eva looked over as Sarah's concerned tone caught their attention.

"I think Boscoe may have discovered a clue to Benjamin's murder. I put it back, but he found a memory card belonging to a camera under Quentin's table, mixed in with his extra pieces that he has in a box underneath it."

The other three women involuntarily glanced over at Quentin's table, but he didn't appear to be aware of anything being amiss. He was talking with a potential customer about a piece they were considering purchasing.

"As soon as I made him drop it into my hand, I got an image of someone removing it from a camera and I have no doubt that it was Benjamin's camera."

"You should call Phil or Dennis right away. They should take this into evidence," Annalise said.

"I hope it won't be a problem that you removed it," Sarah said aloud what Eva and Annalise were already thinking.

"Well, technically, I wasn't the one who removed it. Boscoe was. But I get what you're saying. At least I had my gloves on, so I didn't get my fingerprints on it."

"That was lucky," Eva agreed.

"Would you mind watching Boscoe while I go outside to call the detectives? Obviously, I can't do that in here."

"Of course, Jen. Boscoe will be fine with us, won't you, boy?" Eva said.

He looked up at her and quietly barked once in response.

"Okay, I'll be right back." She bent down to retrieve her phone and walked quickly toward the exit.

"Is everything alright? You look upset."

Jennifer startled when she felt Violet Ouellette's hand on her arm. She'd been so focused on getting to her car to make the call, she hadn't even noticed Violet approach her.

"Yes, I just need to call David. It's nothing to worry about, but I hate making phone calls when I'm out in public. Usually, I'd text but sometimes it's easier to call instead." She looked at Violet, expecting no other explanation was necessary because they'd all been there. She held up her phone indicating she was leaving to make her phone call and once again, headed to her car.

"Dennis, hi! I'm sorry to bother you on a Sunday, but I thought you would want to have this information today. It's about the Benjamin Brooks case."

"It happens that I'm on call today, so no problem. What have you got?"

Jennifer explained how Boscoe had found the memory card and what she'd seen when she held it.

"This Quentin Gray is still there?"

"Yes, the fair won't be over until four o'clock and the vendors have been asked to stay to the end even if they've sold out of what they brought to sell."

"Okay. I'm going to have to give this some thought. We don't have any reason to be searching his things just out of the blue."

"Oh, of course. I didn't think about that. I was so worried about putting it back in his box so you could prove that's where you found it, it didn't occur to me you'd need a reason to search it. That makes perfect sense now. And you can't exactly say you're looking because of what I saw when I held it," Jennifer said, feeling foolish.

"You were right to do that. I'll send you a text if Phil and I figure out a way to handle it."

There's got to be a way to do this, Jennifer thought as she walked back into the cafeteria. A commotion was going on at Quentin's table and all eyes were on him. People were gathered in groups around the room, gawking at the scene playing out.

"Where did you get this?" Bethany was asking as she held the memory card inches away from Quentin's face.

"That's not mine. I don't even know what it is," he defended himself angrily.

"I found it on the floor in front of your table. It's a memory card and I think it belonged to Benjamin Brooks. How come you have it?"

"You're not listening. I told you it's not mine," Quentin said through clenched teeth.

"I'm calling the police!" Bethany turned abruptly, still holding the card, and pulled her phone out of her pocket.

"I never saw that before!" Quentin yelled after her.

Bethany was speaking to someone on her phone and ignored him.

How did that end up on the floor? I'm positive I dropped it into the box. Jennifer hurried over to the Quilts Club table.

"What just happened?"

"Everything was fine and then Bethany started screaming at

Quentin. You came in right as she was winding up and then stormed off," Sarah told her.

"How did it go with the detectives?" Annalise asked.

"Funny you should ask. Dennis told me they couldn't search Quentin's things without a reason and then this happened. It's almost as though someone is pulling some strings to make sure Quentin is implicated."

"I think you're right. I don't know who it is or why, but this plays into the impressions I've been getting all along. There's more than meets the eye going on here," Annalise said.

She looked over at Quentin, who was standing tight-lipped at his table. His face was flushed slightly and his eyes were lowered as he rearranged his display. The people who had been standing at his table moved on to Willow's table, which was next to his. The clusters of people who had been watching went back to what they'd been doing before the drama ensued, but now a dark cloud of energy hung over the room. People here and there took surreptitious glances at Quentin but avoided his table.

Bethany reappeared in the room twenty minutes later followed by Phil Roberts and Dennis Smith. They looked around the room before spotting the Cozy Quilts Club group and acknowledged them with a nod of their heads, but went directly to Quentin's table. They spoke softly, but it was obvious to everyone what was being said when Quentin followed them out of the room. He stopped first at Liam's table, which was beside his, and Liam nodded.

"He must have asked Liam to watch his table," Annalise speculated. "Maybe I should go help him, if that's okay."

"No problem," Eva said. "I think Phil's trying to get your attention, Jen."

Phil was standing in the doorway looking toward them but not making any move to attract attention to himself.

"Can you and Sarah handle things by yourselves?" Jennifer asked.

"We're fine. Go see what he wants," Sarah told her.

As soon as Phil saw Jennifer walking toward him, he went back into the lobby.

"We should go into the principal's office so no one will overhear us," Phil said when Jennifer joined him and then led the way. No one else was in the outer office but Jennifer could hear voices behind the principal's closed door. She couldn't make out the words but Quentin's voice was audible over the others.

"Dennis told me you'd touched the card?"

"Yes. Boscoe took it out of the box. I didn't know what it was so I made him give it to me. That's when I got the images. I couldn't make out a face because my point of view was on the person's hands." She told him about the camera. "I'm certain it wasn't Benjamin holding it, but it was definitely his camera."

"Nothing else?"

"No, I'm sorry. Maybe there's something on the card that will explain it. I'm sure that's why they were taking it out of the camera."

He nodded. "You should probably get back to your table before anyone notices you're in here. If you remember anything else, send me a text."

"I will."

"Well, what did he say?" Eva nearly pounced on Jennifer as soon as she returned.

"Not much. He asked me what I'd seen and how I found the card. I heard Quentin talking in the office with Dennis, and I'm assuming Bethany was with them, but the door was closed, so I couldn't make out the words. From the tone of his voice, though, I could tell Quentin was *not* a happy camper."

CHAPTER 14

Quentin returned a half hour later. Most of the people who'd been there when the detectives had taken him out for questioning had left the building and the new shoppers were unaware of what happened earlier. Despite the rule about vendors not leaving before the end of the day, he began shoving the items he had on display into the boxes under his table. His lips were drawn into a thin line and it didn't take an empath to sense the anger emanating from him.

Liam opened his mouth to speak to him, but Annalise put her hand on his forearm.

"Let him go," she whispered. "This isn't the time to ask questions."

He nodded, knowing she was right.

Quentin loaded his boxes onto the handcart stored behind the table and put on his coat.

"I'm leaving. Obviously. Thanks for watching my table."

"Sure, no problem," Liam said, heeding Annalise's advice not to ask questions now.

"Even when he's dead, Benjamin Brooks manages to mess up my life," Quentin said, bitterly. He nodded a goodbye at Annalise and stalked out of the building.

"Uh oh," Annalise said under her breath. Bethany was coming into the cafeteria and nearly bumped into Quentin as he was leaving. Their voices weren't raised, but their confrontation happened at an unfortunate time when the room was quieter than usual, making it possible for anyone in a twenty-foot radius, including Annalise, to hear their conversation.

"You can't leave now," Bethany said, and attempted to stop him by blocking his way.

"You can't expect me to stay after what just happened. Move out of my way and don't try to stop me."

They faced off in a staring contest, but Bethany was the first to flinch, and she moved aside to let Quentin pass. When she entered the room, she kept her eyes facing forward, not making eye contact with anyone and walked toward the Santa display. The line had dwindled down for the last half hour and no more children were waiting for their turn. Eva watched their interaction, able to guess what it was about when Jim nodded and stood to leave. He gave her a wave as he walked to the lobby.

"Lucky him," she muttered, but Jennifer heard her and sighed.

"Only a couple more hours," she consoled Eva.

Eva smacked her forehead with the palm of her hand. "I completely forgot to tell the detectives about the argument Bethany had with Benjamin. I have to catch them before they leave." She hurried out to the lobby, leaving Jennifer and Sarah wondering what she was talking about. She hadn't told them about this, either.

When Eva reached the lobby, Phil and Dennis were coming out of the principal's office and smiled as soon as they saw her.

"Hello, Eva. Is there anything you can recommend to buy? I haven't bought a gift for my wife yet," Phil said.

"The selection isn't as good as it was a couple hours ago, but you can probably find something. Before you do, though, I have something I need to tell you." She looked back to make sure

Bethany wasn't in the vicinity. "Can we go back to the principal's office?"

The detectives looked at each other and shrugged. They knew from experience that when one of the Quilt Club ladies had information to share, they should listen.

"Sure, right this way."

"What's up?" Dennis asked when they were in the room with the door closed.

"I saw you speaking with Quentin Gray. I don't know if he's in the clear, but I might have another person of interest for you to speak with. I meant to call you about this earlier, but it completely slipped my mind. Too much going on and my memory isn't as sharp as it used to be."

Phil and Dennis waited patiently for Eva to get to the point.

"Anyway, I was talking to Vanessa Barnes. She's the one who does the jewelry. You should definitely check out her pieces. Any of them would make a lovely gift for your wife. But I digress. Vanessa told me she had seen Bethany and Benjamin arguing in the lobby last weekend but stopped when they saw her. Vanessa overheard Bethany tell him she wouldn't let him get away with it." Eva paused to allow them to take this in.

"We'll go talk to her now. Don't worry, we'll make it look innocent, like we're doing our shopping. Which one is Vanessa?" Dennis asked.

"She's to the left of our table. She's the only one selling jewelry. But you should probably talk to her in here. There are too many ears in the cafeteria. I could tell her discreetly that she should report to the principal's office." When they didn't return her smile, she realized they might not have seen the humor of her teacher joke.

Phil cleared his throat. "I see your point. Would you please ask her to come talk to us?"

Her mission accomplished, Eva turned to leave but remembered her intent to get information about their discussion with

Quentin. "Before I go, are you able to tell me what happened with Quentin? I'm sure Jennifer is wondering, too."

"This isn't something to speak about to the general public, but we trust you and the other ladies to keep it in confidence. Quentin claims to have an alibi that places him somewhere else at the time Benjamin was murdered. We'll be checking it out, but for now it looks like he's off the hook," Phil said.

"What about the memory card?"

"We've taken it into evidence and will have our tech guys see what they can retrieve from it. There might be pictures on it that would give us clues about the killer."

Eva's eyes grew round. "If it's not him, the killer could still be here. They have to have planted it in Quentin's box. There's been a rumor circulating around town that they knew each other and had a history."

"That's our guess, too. The murder seems to be personal, so I don't think anyone is in immediate danger, but keep on your toes. It's probably a good thing today is the last day for the craft fair," Phil said.

Eva nodded. "That makes sense. Another reason to be happy when it's over."

"Thanks for the tip, Eva. We'll take it from here. If Vanessa isn't willing to meet with us, would you send us a text, please?" Dennis suggested. "I'll wait in the lobby for her." He reached for the doorknob and was about to open it when Eva stopped him.

"Why don't I leave first. Give me a minute or two before you follow me out," Eva said.

Dennis covered his mouth to hide a smile. Eva caught him, though. *That's rude,* she thought, scowling, and then realized how dramatic she must have sounded. Rather than pursue it, she walked out of the office, closing the door softly behind her. She stopped in the hallway before entering the lobby and peeked out to see if anyone was there, but luck was with her. *Act natural,* she thought and strode into the lobby and back to their table.

"Did you find them?" Jennifer asked.

Annalise gave both of them a curious look. She had returned to their table but wasn't aware that Eva had gone to speak with the detectives.

"I did but I'll have to tell you later," she whispered. She walked to Vanessa's table and whispered the detectives' request to meet with them in the office. Her eyes got round upon hearing it. She didn't respond immediately, but glanced from her table to the room still filled with potential customers.

"I can watch your table for you," Eva told her when she intuited Vanessa's other reason for not wanting to leave.

Vanessa nodded. "Okay. Thanks. If anyone wants to buy something, you can tell them you'll set it aside and I'll be back soon to take their money."

"Of course, dear. I'm happy to."

Fifteen minutes later, Vanessa reappeared in the cafeteria, her cheeks slightly flushed.

"I put aside the pieces like you asked, and the customers said they'd be back to pay for them," Eva told her when she got to the table. "I wrote their names down and put the slip of paper underneath the jewelry they wanted," she said, pointing to several items on top of one of Vanessa's totes.

"Thank you. I was nervous about talking to them, but they were very nice," Vanessa whispered with her back turned to anyone passing by.

"We're neighbors. It's what we do," Eva said, patting Vanessa's shoulder before returning to the Club's table.

Phil and Dennis came into the cafeteria and nonchalantly walked to Abigail's table at the far side of the room. True to their word, they would have appeared to anyone else to be just two more holiday shoppers. *Don't stare at them!* Eva cautioned herself when she looked their way for longer than she might have had she not known what was happening. She could still see them in her peripheral vision and her stomach tensed as they got closer to Vanessa's table. Eva hadn't thought to tell her about her suggestion to act as though they were part of the crowd of shoppers, and was worried Vanessa would think they were coming to question her again. *I might have time to do that now,* she thought, even though they were at Penelope Butler's table next to Vanessa's. Her attention was drawn away, though, when Annalise put her hand on her shoulder.

"Something's going on with Sarah," she whispered into Eva's ear.

They looked over to where Sarah stood motionless, her eyes glazed over. Boscoe began to whine as he stared at the same empty spot where Sarah was looking.

"I think she might be seeing Benjamin," Annalise whispered again.

CHAPTER 15

Sarah blinked and her eyes cleared. She sensed the three sets of eyes of her fellow Club members staring at her, and shook her head to clear it.

"I'll tell you later," she said.

They nodded their understanding. Phil and Dennis appeared at their table, having finished their conversation with Vanessa. Dennis was holding a small bag in his hand.

"Looks like you found something," Eva said, smiling and nodding her head toward his bag.

"I did." He held it up although she had obviously already seen it.

"We still have some lovely items to choose from," Annalise said, cheerily, and making conversation as though they were not already acquainted.

When they reached Sarah's spot, she handed a mug rug to Phil who was the first one in line.

"This is a mug rug. It's bigger than a coaster so you have enough room for a mug *and* a snack. Take a look!" She held his gaze and he nodded as a flash of understanding came to him.

"I'll take it. My wife is always telling me I make a mess on the side table when I have my coffee and cookies while I'm watching TV." He paid Sarah for the mug rug and they moved on their way, stopping at each of the vendors' tables.

"What was that about with Sarah?" Dennis asked Phil when they were in the parking lot.

Phil removed a slip of paper from underneath the oversized coaster.

"She said Benjamin appeared to her and told her we need to examine the photos on the memory card carefully. They have a clue about his killer, but we might not see it right away."

The detectives knew about Sarah's ability to speak with ghosts from the previous cases they'd worked on together.

"Why didn't he just tell her who it is?" Dennis asked.

Phil shrugged. "Who knows?"

"We better get this to the techs ASAP. Maybe they can figure it out."

"That was my plan," Phil replied.

CHAPTER 16

"We did it! The first annual craft fair is officially over," Bethany announced when the last of the shoppers were gone.

Several of the vendors unconsciously performed a synchronized relaxing of their shoulders and let out their breath, including all four Cozy Quilts Club women. They wearily packed up the few remaining unsold items and said their goodbyes to the other vendors.

"Are you sure you're up to having us all come to your house for dinner?" Eva asked.

They had all planned to meet at Annalise's house to celebrate following the craft fair, even before the events that day.

"It's no problem at all. And we've got a lot to talk about," Annalise said.

"I'm going to stop at my house first to drop off Boscoe, but I won't be long," Jennifer told Annalise as she was getting in her car.

"No worries. See you soon!"

"It was so nice of you to plan the post-fair celebration for us, Annalise," Eva said when they were all gathered at Annalise's house. "I didn't realize how hungry I was until I walked in your door and smelled the stew in your crockpot. And is that fresh bread I smell?"

"It is. I fired up the bread maker this morning along with the crockpot."

Sarah's stomach emitted an audible growl which had everyone erupting in laughter.

"I think we must be overtired if that can give us a case of the giggles," Eva said, wiping tears from the corners of her eyes.

"Let's get some food in our bellies. I know we've been sitting most of the day but I'm ready to relax in a more comfortable chair... not that your cushions didn't help, Jen. I was planning to serve buffet style so grab a bowl and dig in. I'll slice the bread and bring it to the table. Would you get the butter out of the fridge, please, Eva?" Annalise said.

Other than an occasional demure slurping sound, the women were quiet as they consumed their dinner.

"My mother always said you know when the food is good when no one is talking," Jennifer said when she had finished.

"Mine, too," Sarah agreed.

"Are we ready to talk about today? We have a lot to discuss, but if no one else is ready yet...?" Annalise let the question hang in the air.

"I'm ready. Why don't you go first, Jen? Tell us about the memory card," Sarah said.

"The image I got was only of the person's hands and they had gloves on so I couldn't tell for sure if it was a man or a woman. I don't think it was Quentin, though."

"That's what the detectives think, too. Phil told me he has an alibi but they're going to verify that. So, the question is, who put it in Quentin's box in the first place?" Eva said.

"And who took it back out and put it on the floor to make sure it got found?" Jennifer asked.

"It's been so frustrating for me that I haven't been able to focus on everything that's been going on. Now that it's over, I might be able to get more insight, no pun intended," Annalise said, smiling at her own joke.

"What had you forgotten to tell the detectives, Eva? You were on a mission when you went to find them," Jennifer said.

"Oh, right! Before we got started this morning… Was it really only this morning? It feels like days ago. Before we got started this morning," Eva began again, "I talked to Vanessa and she told me she saw Bethany and Benjamin arguing last week." Eva told them the rest of the details and the room was quiet as everyone considered this. "That's what I went to tell them, but they didn't say when they're going to speak to Bethany about it."

"Your turn, Sarah," Annalise said. "You saw Benjamin, didn't you?"

"Yes, he appeared to me at Quentin's table. He disappeared too quickly for me to get details, but I slipped a note to Phil with Benjamin's message. He wants them to examine the memory card because there are clues about the killer's identity. Plus, I got a sale out of it," Sarah snickered.

That started another round of giggles.

"You're incorrigible!" Jennifer said through her giggles.

"I'll text him tomorrow and tell him I'll give his money back if he doesn't want to keep it," Sarah said, regaining her composure. "On second thought, I'll give him his money back the next time I see him, and tell him it was a Christmas gift. I should give Dennis one, too. They've both really been good to us."

"They have, haven't they? I'm not sure many other cops would have been as understanding about what we do," Annalise said.

"I think it's been a mutual exchange," Eva said.

"You're right," Sarah said. "Here's to Phil and Dennis," she said, raising her glass.

"Hear, hear," the others responded clinking each other's glass.

"So, what do you think? Should we do this again next year?" Annalise asked.

A moment of silence hung in the air and Annalise thought she might have asked too soon. Eva was the first to reply.

"It was a lot of work, but we'd have a year to plan for it next time. I'm in."

"Me, too," Jennifer said.

"Oh, what the heck? Me, three," Sarah said, but more with resignation than enthusiasm.

"Does this mean I can go to Quilting Essentials tomorrow?" Eva asked, with a mischievous grin.

They all groaned and rolled their eyes.

"'I'm taking that as a yes. Anyone want to join me?"

CHAPTER 17

Annalise smiled when she saw the voice message notification on her phone. This was the first time she'd had a chance to check them since that morning. Her schedule wouldn't normally have been this busy, but she was making up for the time she'd taken off the past three weeks to sew more items to sell at the craft fair.

"I was beginning to think you weren't going to call back," the deep voice on the line rumbled in her ear.

"Sorry. I'm making up for lost time this week and have clients coming in all day."

"I missed not seeing you last night."

"Me, too. The ladies and I needed to do a debrief. You're not going to believe it, but I even got them to commit to doing it again next year!"

Liam chuckled. "You do have a way of making people want to be with you, so I'm not surprised. Speaking of which, do you have time this week to meet for dinner? Your choice of the night. I'm free all week. Well, I may not be free, but I am available."

"You didn't really say that, did you?" she teased.

"Yeah, I guess that was pretty cheesy," he admitted, sheepishly. "But seriously, do you have time?"

"How about Thursday? After being around so many people during the craft fair, I need some alone time to decompress."

"I understand."

She caught the disappointment in his voice and was going to suggest meeting earlier in the week, but caught herself. *Don't do it, Annalise. Don't fall into the trap of agreeing to do something you're not ready to do just to make someone else happy at your expense.*

"I should take that advice, too. Most of the time I'm working by myself so it's been a lot to have so much sensory stimulation. Now that I'm saying that out loud, I realize a break to recharge my battery is what I need."

"Have you ever had a Reiki session?" Annalise asked.

"No, but when you have an opening on your calendar, I'd like to schedule a session. In the meantime, I'll listen to my meditation playlist and count the days until Thursday."

"You're laying it on pretty thick tonight," she teased again.

"You say smarm, I say charm… I did it again, didn't I?"

"Yup."

"I better say goodbye and hang up or you're going to reconsider altogether. You have a good rest of the day. I'll see you Thursday."

Is this going too fast? Are you sure you're ready for more than friendship? I really like him, but this is a little scary, too. Following Liam's lead, she went to her sitting room and looked through her CDs. In her treatment room, she streamed the music, but here she was still old-school. Picking one, she placed it in the CD player and sat in her comfy chair, wrapping herself in the softness of the knit throw draped on the arm of the chair. She'd dimmed the lights and it wasn't long before she fell asleep, all of the stress of the past weeks catching up to her. And dreamed.

CHAPTER 18

J ust *onnne more second.* Sarah finished typing the email she was working on, hit Send, and picked up her ringing phone, her eyes still on her monitor screen.

"Sarah Pascal."

"Sarah, it's Phil Roberts. I wanted to let you know that our techs were able to pull up the photos on the memory card. It has to be the one that was missing from Benjamin Brooks' camera. All of the photos are from the craft fair. We've had a chance to look them over, but nothing is out of the ordinary for what we would expect to be seeing."

"Huh. I was sure that's what he told me, *We should look at the photos.* I guess I could have been mistaken. Our connection didn't last long, so that's possible. He may have had more to say but didn't get the chance."

"We'll go through them again, but if he pays you another visit, let us know."

"I will. By the way, did Quentin Gray's alibi check out?" Sarah asked.

"It did. He was in the security footage with his bowling team right where he said he was, so we're back to square one."

"I'm not surprised. I'd never met him until the craft fair, but he didn't strike me as the murdering kind."

"That still leaves the question of who put the card in his box. They obviously were hoping to point the finger at him. And the other question is who took it out of the box and dropped it on the floor to make sure someone found it after Jennifer put it back."

"We were wondering the same thing. I can't say for sure, but I suspect it might have been Benjamin. He's trying to help us."

"Could you contact him to ask who did it?"

Sarah heard the hesitation in Phil's voice, but wasn't sure if it was because he thought he was overstepping or because he was embarrassed by the idea of a police detective asking someone to contact a ghost for information. She covered her mouth to stifle a chuckle. *Should I tease him about this?* She almost did, but changed her mind. Phil had a sense of humor, but this might not be the time to put it to the test.

"I'm not sure, Phil. I don't sense his presence around me, but that doesn't mean it's not possible to make contact. It's not a good time right now. I have a project that's due today. I promise I'll give it a try as soon as I can, though."

"Thanks, Sarah."

"You're welcome, Phil."

"And, Sarah? Thanks for not giving me a hard time about asking you to talk to Benjamin even though you wanted to."

Her jaw dropped, but he disconnected before she had time to respond.

"What do you think about that, Max?" she asked. Max was asleep in his dog bed beside her desk but lifted his head when he heard his name. "Phil might be a psychic, too."

Nonplussed, Max laid his head back on the cushion and went back to sleep.

CHAPTER 19

*G*loved hands were holding a camera. Images flashed by, too quickly to see the detail. An image would pause only long enough on some for the person's fingers to push the trash can icon, and then move on to the next. When they were done, they removed the memory card and put the camera back in the bag on the luggage rack and left the room.

Annalise's eyelids fluttered. The CD had stopped playing and the silence of the room and dim light combined with the residual images of her dream made her shiver involuntarily. She closed her eyes again, hoping to replay the dream in her mind to get more clarity, but it was a futile exercise. *It doesn't matter. I know what happened. I need to call Sarah.*

She checked her watch and was surprised to see it had only been an hour. *The silence when the CD stopped playing must have woken me,* she thought. It wasn't too late to call Sarah now. Picking up her phone, she touched the screen for Sarah's number and was rewarded with an answer after only two rings.

"Hi, Annalise. Did you know Phil is psychic, too?"

"Phil is what?" Annalise was confused by the question and thought she must still be fuzzy from her dream.

Sarah laughed, and then told her about Phil's call earlier.

Annalise laughed along with her. "It's my belief that everyone is psychic, but not everyone is tuned into their abilities. And like anything else, some people are more gifted than others. I could play the piano if I took lessons, but it wouldn't come as naturally as it would to someone who is born with the gift."

"That makes sense. Sorry, I got us off-track. I'm guessing you called with something to tell me."

"I did. I had a dream that the person who stole the memory card deleted photos before they took the card. I can't explain why they would do that if they intended to take the card anyway. Can you?"

"It's easier to do it when the card is still in the camera. You can do it afterwards, but it's more hoops to jump through. They were probably hoping that even if the card was found, whatever they didn't want to be seen on the photos would be gone. It also makes sense now why Phil wasn't able to see anything suspicious about them that would lead to the killer's identity," Sarah said.

"Oh, that clears that up. Is it possible to retrieve deleted photos like they can do for files on a computer?"

"I'm not a hundred percent sure about that, but my guess is that Benjamin had a cloud account as a backup. If he was able to upload his photos before the killer got to the card, any of the missing ones would be there." Sarah paused to think. "That's exactly what I need to do, Annalise. I need to find his cloud account. It will take me some time since I don't have a place to start without knowing anything about his accounts."

"But not impossible?"

"Don't you remember? I'm Super Sleuth Sarah," she teased. It was a moniker she'd given herself the month before when she'd found evidence that proved a killer had used a fake company to embezzle money from the law firm where he worked.

Annalise laughed. "How could I have forgotten that?"

"I'm going to start looking now. This has me excited to see what I can find. I love a challenge."

"If anyone can do it, it's Super Sleuth Sarah. Let me know if... I'm sorry, when... you find something."

"You'll be the first!"

CHAPTER 20

Ashley knocked on the doorframe of Sarah's office before entering so she wouldn't startle her. Sarah was engrossed in a collage of photos on her monitor and didn't hear Ashley approach. "Are you going to come to bed?"

Despite her warning knock, Sarah jumped when she heard Ashley's voice.

"What time is it?" Sarah asked.

"It's ten thirty. You've been up here ever since we finished dinner. What are you looking for anyway?"

Sarah told her about Annalise's dreams and their connection to Benjamin's murder. "It didn't take me as long as I thought it might to find his cloud account. I'll need to check with Phil to ask him how many photos were on the memory card and compare that with this file to figure out if Annalise was right. Even so, I've been over the photos a few times and I can't see anything that would have been a reason to kill Benjamin to get them."

"Maybe you'll have better luck after a good night's sleep and fresh eyes in the morning," Ashley suggested.

Sarah sighed. "You're right. You know how I hate to give up until I've solved the puzzle, though."

"I do, but it will still be here tomorrow."

"Yes, mom. I'll be right there," Sarah said, using her best annoyed kid voice.

"Nope. If you're going to use the mom ploy to guilt me that I'm treating you like a child, I'm going to wait here while you shut things down." Ashley stood with her arms crossed over her chest.

Sarah frowned at her, but turned back to the computer and shut it down for the night.

"Come on, Max. Mom's being mean and making us go to bed."

Max jumped up from his bed, where he'd already been asleep and followed the women, tail wagging, and oblivious to the scene that had just played out.

CHAPTER 21

"Phil, it's Sarah. Would your techs be able to make a copy of the memory card so you could bring it to show me? I might be able to see something that you didn't." She wasn't being completely honest about her motives. *I'll explain it when he gets here,* she argued with her conscience.

"Why don't you come down to the station and I can show you here?"

This isn't going to be as easy as I'd hoped. I'm going to have to confess the real reason I want him to come here.

"I have something else I need to show you and it would be better if I did it at my computer, if you get my drift."

"I'm not going to ask. I'll check with them about making the copy and let you know when Dennis and I can bring it by. Will you be available all day?"

"Today is a rare day without any meetings, so anytime would work for me," she said.

That was fast! she said when her phone displayed his name half an hour later.

"We can be there in fifteen minutes," he said, when she answered.

"Great! I'll be ready." She hid the application on her screen for the project she was working on and brought up the photos she'd downloaded from Benjamin's cloud account while she waited for them to arrive.

Max jumped up from his bed and began barking. Before she could stop him, he ran down the stairs, barking as he went, and stood in front of the entry door with Sarah on his heels. She put her fingers under his collar and gently pulled him back so she could open the door for the detectives.

"Max! It's just Phil and Dennis. You can stand down."

He stopped barking and looked up at her to make sure she really meant it. As soon as the detectives walked through the door, his tail began wagging furiously when he recognized them, and Sarah removed her fingers from his collar so he could greet them.

"Good job, Max. You would have scared me away," Phil told him as he bent down to pat Max's head.

Max went to Dennis, standing next to Phil, expecting a similar reward from him. Dennis scratched Max under his ears. Max responded by looking up at Dennis adoringly, in total bliss.

"Alright, it's time for the detectives and me to go to work. Go lay down like a good boy," Sarah told him. He obliged instantly, bounding up the stairs ahead of them.

"What's this?" Phil demanded when he spied the photos on Sarah's monitor.

"It's what I didn't want to tell you about on the phone," Sarah said. "I want to compare these photos that I got from the cloud…"

"Stop right there. We don't want to know," Dennis said, holding up his hand.

"Not a problem. The reason I asked you to bring a copy of the photos you have is because Annalise had a dream. In it, the person who took the memory card was using the camera to delete some of the photos before they stole the card. We think if we compare the photos and any are missing, it might be a clue about who the killer is."

"What if they're all the same?" Phil asked.

"It might just be a waste of time. It doesn't make sense that the person who planted the card in Quentin's box would have left incriminating photos on it, though."

Phil handed her the flash drive and she plugged it into her computer. She used her second monitor to display the two sets of photos, the ones from the flash drive on one monitor and the cloud's on the other. They went through each one and four were in the file Sarah found on the cloud that the detectives didn't have.

"Why would these have been deleted?" They don't look like any big deal," Dennis said.

Sarah sat quietly, scrutinizing the missing photos she'd found. They hadn't jumped out at her when she'd examined them earlier, but now, it made sense.

"I think I know the answer to that."

CHAPTER 22

"You do?" Phil asked.

"I still don't understand what the killer thought was so damaging but there's more to the story of what happened when those pictures were taken." She pointed to the one taken at Fiona Walsh's table in which Fiona's eyebrows were knit together and her lips were drawn in a tight line. "Fiona claimed that someone had stolen some of her things and was spouting off that Bethany should have done a better job of securing our stuff overnight. And in this photo," she pointed to the group picture at Sophia Peterson's table, "one of Sophia's paintings had been slashed." Next, she directed their attention to the pictures taken the day of Willow Stone's allergic reaction to the peanuts. There were several showing a group of onlookers at Willow's table and the first responders assisting her. "Willow is allergic to peanuts but Nathan, he's the one at this table," she pointed to him, "didn't know that and was snacking on a bag of peanuts. That might not be directly connected, but Annalise has been telling us something more is going on than is obvious on the surface. I wouldn't be surprised if we find out it wasn't completely Nathan's fault about the peanuts."

"Okay, I get where you're going with this, but who is the

person who connects the dots to them?" Dennis asked, looking from one picture to the next.

"It doesn't mean she killed Benjamin or even that she's the one who stole the memory card, but look here, here, and here. You can't see her face in this one because she's not facing the camera and most of her body is obstructed by the tablecloth," she pointed to a figure crouched down by Fiona's table, "and now look here and here." In both sets of photos, the clothing matched. "When they were deleting the pictures, they must have skimmed over these and didn't realize how they could be tied to them. They weren't planning on anyone finding the missing photos to compare them and put two and two together about being the common denominator with the incidents at the fair."

A flash of comprehension passed over the detectives' faces and they nodded their heads in agreement when Sarah finished.

"We're going to need more evidence to tie them to the murder, but it's a really good lead, Sarah. We wouldn't have made the connection without your help," Phil said.

Dennis nodded his head in confirmation. "Not in a million years."

"And Annalise. If she hadn't told me about her dream, I wouldn't have looked for Benjamin's cloud account. We make a good team."

"Yes, we do."

"Wait, didn't she show up on the hotel's security tapes?" Sarah asked when she realized they hadn't mentioned those.

Phil sighed. "The camera for that floor had gone on the fritz earlier that day and there was a mix-up in getting the order in to have it fixed. They didn't realize it hadn't happened until we asked for the tapes. Talk about getting lucky or unlucky, from our perspective."

"It wasn't knocked out intentionally?"

"No, they checked. It hadn't been tampered with," Dennis said.

"Now that you know who to narrow it down to look for, is it

worth going through the tapes for the common areas? Not trying to do your job, just asking," Sarah held up her hand to ward off any rebukes.

"Already thought of that and was going to suggest it, but you beat me to it," Phil said, but he was smiling, so Sarah knew she hadn't offended him.

"Would you mind printing out a copy of this photo? I'd like to take it with me to show to the hotel staff," Dennis asked.

"Of course!" Sarah queued up the photo and handed him the printout.

"Thanks. This will save us some time. We'll see ourselves out," Dennis said, giving Max a pat on the head before he and Phil left.

Max looked at Sarah, but when he was sure she wasn't leaving with the detectives, he flopped his head back down on his bed.

Sarah picked up her phone, excited to finally have them leave so she could send a text to the Club.

> You aren't going to believe this, but I think the detectives and I figured out Violet is involved. She might not be the one who actually killed Benjamin, but she's connected somehow. You were right about pictures being missing, Annalise. They all pointed toward Violet being the link.

The responses came within seconds.

EVA

Wow!

JENNIFER

ANNALISE

Did not see that coming!

No cracks about a psychic not knowing
something in advance!! 😄

CHAPTER 23

"How can I assist you today?" the clerk at the Registration desk in the lobby of the hotel asked. He was a twenty-something young man wearing what came across as a genuine smile. His name tag identified him as Tim Wright.

"Well, Tim, we'd like to speak with the manager," Phil said, and discreetly held his badge palmed in his hand so that only the clerk could see it. Dennis did the same.

"Oh, yes! Of course," the now flustered clerk replied. He punched one of the buttons on the telephone at his station and turned his back to them. "There are two police officers here who would like to speak with you." He spoke into the phone's receiver, just above a whisper, and then turned back around, placing it into its cradle.

"She'll be right with you." The jaunty smile was back. "If you wouldn't mind taking a seat in the lounge area while I assist these arrivals." He pointed toward the seats scattered around the lobby and a gas fireplace, its imitation logs glowing from the flames shooting up around it, centered on the wall. When they looked in that direction, they noticed the couple behind them waiting to check in.

It didn't take long for the manager to walk out of an office door behind the reception area. She was a tall, blonde woman in a navy pantsuit and white blouse. The name, Harper Hughes, was emblazoned on a gold-colored name badge pinned to her jacket.

"Why don't we discuss how I can help you in my office? Follow me." She turned and walked in the direction from which she'd arrived before asking them to identify themselves.

Phil and Dennis exchanged glances and rose to follow her, realizing she didn't want any curious onlookers in the lobby to know she had two policemen there on official business. The office was small, but neat. Her desk did not have any paperwork on its surface and the credenza behind her had a real potted plant, not silk, a printer, and photos of a man and two young children, presumably her family. The artwork on the walls was the typical hotel landscape variety. When they were seated in the guest chairs facing her desk and the door closed behind them, only then did she speak.

"How can I help you… ?" she paused, waiting for them to introduce themselves.

They each stated their names and pulled a business card from their jacket pockets which they handed to her. Dennis nodded to Phil to speak.

"We're assigned to the Benjamin Brooks homicide. We're aware the cameras weren't working on that floor the night of the murder, but we haven't seen the security tapes for the lobby, and any public doorways, or the parking lot. Would it be possible to take a look at those now?"

"That's not a problem," she said, and her shoulders visibly relaxed.

Dennis pulled the photo Sarah had printed from his pocket and unfolded it before placing it on her desk. "We'd also like to ask your staff if they remember seeing this woman on the premises. Are any of the ones who were on duty that day here now?"

"I'll have to check the schedule. Could I make a copy? I can check later with any who aren't here today and get back to you."

"That would be appreciated. And if you could send us a list of their names? Just in case we need to follow up," he added.

She paused, unsure whether to agree. "I think that will be possible," she said after a moment. She turned to make a copy of the photo and handed the original back to Dennis. "I'll let Security know we'll be coming and have them get the tapes ready. What are the dates you'll need?" She repeated the information to the clerk who answered her call.

"He should have those pulled by the time we get to his office." She rose, and walked around her desk to open the door, indicating they should follow. She walked to a door marked Employees Only and slid a plastic keycard into the slot; the same system used for the guest rooms. The light turned green and she opened the door into a small hallway in which a break room and lockers were on one side and on the other was a closed door marked Security. Once again, she slid her card into the lock and the light turned green.

"Do you have the tapes ready, Brian?" she asked the gray-haired man sitting at a desk, his ample belly stretching the limits of the buttonholes of his shirt to nearly the breaking point. Three rows of monitors in front of him were currently active and displaying the common areas, parking lot, and hallways for the four floors in the building. A separate monitor displayed a still image of the lobby with the date they'd requested imprinted along the bottom.

"Yes, ma'am. All queued up."

"These are Detectives Roberts and Smith. They're investigating the death of our guest, Benjamin Brooks. I'll leave you to assist them, but if you need me for anything else, you can call my office number. Gentlemen," she bid her goodbye and left them to their task.

"Is there a particular time you want me to start?" Brian asked.

Phil pulled out a small wire bound notebook and flipped through the pages. "Try running it from four p.m. the night his body was found. If we don't see what we're looking for, we might have to go back."

Brian fast forwarded the tape to the four o'clock time stamp, overshooting it by five minutes and rewound to the right time. "Do you want it to just play, or, if you want, I can increase the speed in increments?"

"Let's see what it looks like at the two setting," Phil suggested. "We were told there's no footage for the floor Mr. Brooks was staying in because there were some technical issues with the camera. Is that correct?"

"Yeah, sorry about that. We had a snafu with the work order. Do you want to look at the other floors, though?"

"Run the common areas first. If we see what we're looking for, we can go from there," Phil said.

The room was quiet as the three men watched the images scroll by until Dennis came to attention. "Stop! Run it back thirty seconds." Brian reversed the tape. "There." He pointed to a woman walking through the lobby toward the bank of elevators. She was wearing a hat that was pulled down, obscuring the top half of her face.

Phil looked at Dennis with his eyebrows scrunched and then shrugged his shoulders with his palms up.

"I recognize that outfit from the photos. She wore it at the craft fair. I can't remember which day, but I'm positive it's the same one," he answered Phil's unspoken question. Now, he took out his notebook, and marked down the time on the video. "Okay, keep going," he told Brian.

By the time the video of the lobby had run past the estimated time of the murder by two hours, Dennis told Brian he could stop the recording. Either the woman had stayed longer than he'd estimated or she'd left by taking the stairs.

"Okay, now run the video for any of your exits that don't go through the lobby." He glanced down at his notebook and gave Brian the time they'd first seen the woman. "Start there first."

At the time stamp two hours later, the door leading to the parking lot opened and she exited the building. By this time, it was dark, but a light illuminated the doorway. "There she is! Now, can you expand the view so we can see which car she goes to?"

Brian changed the point of view to the parking lot at that time and they watched as she walked hastily to an SUV and got in. "Can you zoom in on the license plate?" Phil asked. He didn't have much hope it would work even with zooming in and the parking lot wasn't lit well in the area where the car was parked.

"I'll try but I can't promise it will be clear." He zoomed in, but as Phil feared, it was too dark and the video became too grainy to read the plate number.

Dennis and Phil's excitement at being able to connect the car to Violet deflated.

"Well, at least we've got the make and model of the car. We can check registrations to see if she owns one like it," Phil said.

"You're right. It's still a lead. Brian, can you make us a copy of those and email them to me?"

"I can do better if you don't mind waiting five minutes, maybe less," Brian said, grinning up at Dennis. "I can put them onto a flash drive for you."

"While you're at it, could you take a screenshot of the woman as she's walking by the Registration desk and print a copy?"

"Yeah, I can do that."

"Thanks, much appreciated."

"Always happy to help our men in blue… or suits," he amended since they were not wearing uniforms.

Dennis filled in the information needed on a small evidence bag while they waited and Brian dropped the device inside when it was done.

"Wait, we should ask if the desk clerk was on duty that day and show him the photos," Dennis said, reaching out to grab Phil's arm to stop him just as they were about to exit the building. "He's probably the only one who might have seen her. That's why I asked Brian to print out that screenshot. It looked like she walked right over to the elevators as soon as she came in and then left by the back door, so not much sense wasting our time with any of the other staff."

"Might as well, while we're here."

The clerk looked up from his computer as he noticed them approaching, a big smile on his face which vanished as soon as he recognized them. It was replaced with a wary look, but he managed to smile politely, although not with the same enthusiasm.

"Hello, again, Tim. We're wondering if you were on duty the night of the… recent incident?" Dennis asked. He'd been about to say murder, but thought better of it.

"Yes, I was," Tim said, still wary.

Dennis pulled the photo of Violet out of his pocket and laid it on the countertop. "Did you see this woman come through the lobby that night?"

"No, I don't recall seeing her."

"How about this one?" He handed her the one Brian had printed for them.

Tim picked up the photo and studied it before handing it back to Dennis. "Yes, I did. That big hat caught my attention. I asked if I could help her, but she walked right past me without answering. She didn't even look at me and headed straight for the elevators so I figured she must be visiting a guest or someone else had checked her in earlier. I had the night shift so I'd only been on duty about an hour."

"Could you see her face at all?" Phil asked.

"No, sorry. Like I said, she had that big floppy hat on and it hid her face."

"Did she come back through the lobby on her way out?"

"Now that you mention it, no, she didn't. I didn't think

anything of it because she could have been visiting a friend and stayed overnight. That happens."

Disappointed, Dennis folded up the photo and put it back in his pocket.

"Thanks, anyway, Tim. That was still helpful," Dennis said.

Tim beamed with the praise, more relaxed now.

They each handed him one of their cards. "In case you think of anything later," Phil said.

"It was worth a shot," Dennis said.

"All in all, though, not a bad day," Phil said as they walked back to their car.

CHAPTER 24

"Oh, look! Penelope Butler just came in. Should we invite her over?" Annalise asked. She was having lunch at the Diner with Eva and Jennifer.

"That's a great idea," Eva said, turning to peek over the top of the booth behind her.

Annalise waved, catching Penelope's attention. "Come join us!"

Penelope acknowledged her with a smile and walked toward their booth.

"Come sit beside me," Eva said, sliding over to make room.

"Thanks. I was going to order takeout because I hate eating by myself in restaurants, but this is much nicer."

"Have you recovered from the craft fair?" Jennifer asked.

"It took me a couple days to recover from it, but I've replaced that stress with the last-minute shopping, wrapping, and baking I didn't have time for during the fair."

Betty appeared at their booth wearing a Santa hat and a candy cane pin on her blouse, adding to the festive atmosphere. The diner was decorated in full holiday splendor. The windows had been stenciled with holiday scenes using canned fake snow. The tables and booths had small centerpieces made of silk poinsettias and garlands of plastic greenery were strung along the backs of the booth top dividers. They'd even set up an artificial Christmas tree in one corner with slips of paper clipped to it and wrapped gifts under the tree. The slips of paper had a gift wish written on it by a needy local family, mostly children, but some elderly residents as well, identified only with a number. People could select a slip and once they brought in the requested gift already wrapped, it would be placed under the tree along with its number. It had all been arranged by a local charity so even Betty didn't know who the recipients were. On Christmas Eve, they would collect the gifts and deliver them to the homes of the families. Music wasn't usually part of the diner's ambience but during this season, they made an exception and the typical playlist of holiday music provided an accompaniment to the conversations.

Betty set down another place setting and glass of water in front of Penelope. "Ho, ho, ho, ladies. Do you need more time?" The words were meant to be cheery, but weren't reflected in Betty's body language and tone of voice. The implication subtext was *I'm being told I have to say ho, ho, ho but don't expect me to like it.*

"We've decided, but how about you, Penny? You just got here," Annalise asked.

"I knew what I wanted when I came in, so I'm ready now."

"Did you have a good experience at the fair? Good enough to do it again next year?" Annalise picked up the conversation once Betty had taken their orders. Betty hadn't engaged in her usual chit-chat and it was clear to everyone that the holiday rush, and probably the constant exposure to the music, was getting on her nerves.

"I think so," she said, bobbing her head. "There was more drama than I was expecting, but I can't imagine it would be that way every year."

"If a murder happened every year that was connected to the

craft fair, I don't think it would draw many vendors," Jennifer agreed. "Not to mention all the other things going on."

"That probably wouldn't happen if Violet wasn't involved," Penny stated matter-of-factly. "The other stuff, not the murder," she added. "Well, that doesn't sound right either. I didn't mean Violet had anything to do with the murder, just the drama at the fair."

"Oh? How so?" Eva asked.

"Bethany told me Violet wanted to have her own table but Bethany turned her down. I can't prove it, but if you told me she's the one who took Fiona's things, it wouldn't surprise me." ·

Jennifer and Eva both raised their eyebrows, but Annalise appeared lost in thought, as if Penny's words had struck a chord.

"You remember how she's always been, Annalise. We grew up together," Penny explained for Jennifer's and Eva's benefit. "She was always jealous of Sophia, Fiona, and Marylou's talents. I could picture her doing it to get back at Fiona and cause trouble for Bethany."

"Who's Marylou?" Jennifer asked.

"Oh, right, you're too young to know that history. She's an artist, too, but she doesn't live in Glen Lake anymore.. She was a bit wild in her younger days and went off to join a commune. It was the late sixties or early seventies. Doesn't matter. She decided to change her name because she never liked the name Marylou and Violet knew that. She goes by Destiny now and she's Willow's mother. Willow didn't grow up in Glen Lake, but decided to move here about ten years ago, I think."

"You're right, I was not aware of that," Jennifer said.

"Neither did I, or I'd forgotten it. We knew each other, but it was more an acquaintance than friends relationship. I had no idea Willow is her daughter."

"What about Sophia's painting? Do you think she did that, too?" Eva asked.

"That might be going too far even for Violet. Didn't she find a rough spot on the easel it was on? I thought that's why it got torn," Penny said.

Betty arrived with their meals, interrupting the conversation. "Can I get you anything else?" she said in a tone that left no doubt it wasn't an actual request and almost dared them to ask. She was rewarded with four variations of no thanks, and slapped their tabs down on the table.

"Wow, I've never seen Betty act like this. Is she okay?" Jennifer whispered, not wanting Betty to hear and incur her wrath.

Annalise watched Betty's retreating back, striding purposefully toward another diner's table. "I think she's got something on her mind. It's a personal problem she needs to work out."

Her comment didn't surprise the others, but Penny cocked her head slightly to the side as she looked at Annalise, although she kept her thoughts to herself.

"I should get going anyway, but that sounded like a hint to leave to me," Penny said, picking up her tab. "Thanks for inviting me to sit with you. Maybe we can do this again sometime."

They waited until she was out the door before returning to their conversation about the craft fair.

"Sarah has to be right about Violet. This points the finger at her even more. You know her, Annalise. Do you think Violet really could be behind all of this?" Jennifer asked.

"I haven't seen a lot of her since we graduated. We were never close and I didn't make a conscious effort to keep in touch. What Penny said about Violet being jealous was right on the money, and she could be mean-spirited and vindictive. That had a lot to do with why I kept my distance, then and now," Annalise said. "Penny might be right about Violet being the one who took Fiona's things. It's like I've been saying all along that my spidey senses were tingling throughout the whole fair."

"And what happened with Sophia and Willow?" Eva asked.

Annalise considered that. "Now that I know Bethany turned

her down for a table, I can imagine it being true. She was right there when the painting was slashed and when Willow had her allergic reaction, but I didn't think much of it at the time because she was a volunteer. I'd hate to think she would put Willow's life in danger, though. If she did somehow do it, she must have luck on her side to have Nathan bring peanuts in so it would draw attention to him."

"What if it wasn't all luck? Did Nathan bring them in himself or did she just happen to give them to him?" Eva asked.

"I hadn't thought of that. Maybe we could ask. We could visit his shop," Jennifer suggested.

Annalise and Eva exchanged glances. "Let's do it!" they said at the same time.

At the cash register with their tabs, Betty was in a better mood, almost as though a cloud had lifted. She greeted them with her usual smile and cheerful demeanor.

"Everything okay today, Betty?" Annalise asked, keeping her tone light.

Betty frowned. "I'm fine. It's that Penelope Butler. She's the worst gossip!"

The irony of Betty being upset about someone else being a gossip was almost too much. Eva and Jennifer, standing behind Annalise, looked down at the floor and covered their mouths to hide their smiles. Annalise had to literally bite her tongue to keep her expression neutral. They held it together until they were in the parking lot.

"Talk about the pot calling the kettle black!" Eva said, between giggles.

"Oh, I needed that after all the depressing talk about Violet. Do we still want to talk to Nathan?" Jennifer asked.

"I think we have to. If for no other reason than to put it to rest one way or the other," Annalise said. "I'll meet you there."

CHAPTER 25

As was the case with many of Glenburn's mom and pop businesses, Nathan's was located on his home property. He had converted the former barn into a combination studio and retail shop with supplies for making stained glass projects, along with items he'd made. He also taught classes and did custom work.

A bell chimed announcing their arrival when they opened the door. Panes of colorful glass were stacked vertically in cubbies, sorted by colors and types of glass in one section of the room. Windows and skylights had been added to the barn to allow more light into the building. Nathan had also set up two light boxes so customers could audition glass to see how it would look with light shining through. The colors could appear completely different when held up to the light. Lamp shades, some in Tiffany style, were hung throughout the shop space. Smaller items such as candle holders, lamps, and other decorative pieces were displayed on shelving. In some of the windows, panels were hung with small chains so that the sunshine coming through them created speckles of color on the floor and displays. Dozens of tiny rainbows were visible as well from those that had prisms in their designs.

"Well, hello, ladies. I didn't expect to see you so soon," Nathan greeted them as he came into the shop from the rear of the building.

"We were just having lunch and talking about you," Annalise said. "It was such a hectic time at the fair that I didn't have a chance to look over your things as much as I wanted, so here we are."

"It's so pretty here. I love how the light comes through the glass. It makes me happy seeing all the colors," Eva said, still looking around the room at the displays.

"You picked a perfect day to visit. It's not quite as colorful when it's overcast."

"Do you still have any of the small lights that had the shades set in the brass stands? The ones that you can switch out for different occasions or when you want to change your décor?" Jennifer asked.

"I know exactly what you mean, and yes. They're right over here."

The women followed him to the display.

"They're mostly holiday themed that I have on display now but I have others I can show you."

"These are lovely," Eva said. "I don't know how I missed them at the fair. "And you can change them?"

"Here, let me show you." Nathan lifted the glass out of the slot in the base and replaced it with one stored behind it. "Voila!"

"You may have just found yourself a repeat customer. I can see myself coming back for all the holidays."

"We were comparing notes about the fair earlier. What did you think about it? Do you think it was worth your time?" Annalise asked, segueing into the real reason they'd come to the shop.

"Oh, yes! Other than my giving Willow an allergic reaction and nearly putting her into anaphylactic shock." Nathan's face took on a remorseful expression. "I wasn't thinking when I ate the peanuts."

"Did anyone tell you about Willow's allergy ahead of time?" Annalise asked.

"No, or I certainly wouldn't have been eating them. I'm surprised Violet didn't know either, what with her being a volunteer, and all."

The women's eyes met briefly.

"Violet?" Annalise encouraged him to go on.

"Yes. She's the one who gave them to me. She had stopped at my table to ask if I needed anything and I mentioned that I was starving, but I forgot to bring any snacks. She offered to get me something and that's what she brought back."

"Everything turned out okay. That's the important thing," Eva said.

"I told Willow how sorry I was and she was very kind about it. She didn't blame me at all." His shoulders relaxed, but he seemed anxious to move on to other topics.

"Would you like me to ring that up for you?" he asked Eva.

"Yes, please. I'd like to look around at some of your other things, too."

"You go right ahead. I'll get this wrapped up for you in the meantime. And if I can help either of you, just give me a shout," he said to Jennifer and Annalise.

"I'd like this one," Jennifer said, pointing to one on the shelf. "I remember it from the craft fair and was hoping you'd still have it."

"Of course!" He removed it from the shelf and carried both to the checkout stand and began wrapping the shades in layers of paper.

"I won't take long," Eva told them after he'd gone. "I thought it might be less obvious if we didn't leave as soon as he told us about Willow," she said, keeping her voice low.

"No problem. I saw a piece I'd like to buy for my treatment room. This has turned out to be worth the trip in more ways than one," Annalise said, winking.

CHAPTER 26

You really made a mess in here.

Annalise stood in the doorway of her sewing room with her hands on her hips, surveying the piles of fabric scraps on the table that she had used for cutting out her projects. They were too big to throw away and now that she knew about crumb quilting, she was saving even more of the scraps than she had in the past. All her Reiki sessions were done for the day and she was determined to clean up the fabric detritus. At first, a sense of overwhelm had her thinking about turning around to snuggle up on the couch and finish the book she was reading instead, but she knew she'd regret it later.

Start with the bigger pieces first and get those folded. Sorting through the piles and pulling out the larger ones made sense. In less than ten minutes those were all folded into a neat pile. Next were the ones big enough to cut into standard pre-cut size block sizes, starting with ten-inch squares and working her way down to two and a half inch squares for the smallest pieces. Any left-over pieces from this were tossed in a heap to be added to her crumb quilt stash once she made her way through what was remaining in the original piles still unsorted. Christmas music was playing in the background and she hummed along with it as she worked. *I was beginning to think I wouldn't want to listen to Christmas music again until next year after hearing it so much during the craft fair,* she thought, smiling.

She was about to put everything in a tote to pack away, but remembered her own advice to make more items throughout the year to sell at next year's craft fair, *assuming there is one.* To do that, she'd need to have the fabric close at hand. *I might be able to listen to the music, but I just don't have it in me today to do more holiday sewing.* She put the cover on the tote and tucked it under the table instead. She picked up the rulers and rotary cutters and hung them on the pegboard on her wall.

When she picked up the scissors, her body stiffened. *This must be what happens to Jennifer,* she thought, as a wave of awareness flowed through her. She wasn't seeing images the way Jennifer did, but the impression that the weapon Benjamin's killer had used was a pair of scissors was too strong to ignore. *I need to tap into this now while the sensation is so strong.* She started to put the scissors back on the table, but decided to take them with her instead, thinking it might help her keep the connection. Just like she knew that going to her sitting room was where she needed to be. She sat in her chair, held the scissors in her lap, and closed her eyes.

Benjamin was coming out of the bathroom of his hotel room, swaying slightly as though he was having difficulty keeping his balance.

"Whadder ya doin' wif my camra?" The words were slurred, and Annalise knew he'd been drugged. *"You put somfing in my drink."*

He stood still, blinking his eyes to stay awake but his head continued to nod slowly up and down as he fought the fatigue taking over his body. With a great deal of effort, he opened his eyes wide and willed himself to stand straight, then began to walk again. He took a few steps forward and stumbled.

Annalise was looking at him from the point of view of the other person in his room. She wasn't sure if it was intuition that told her it was a woman or if she'd been influenced by the knowledge Violet was the likely suspect. Benjamin's hands reached out instinctively, knowing he was falling. Too late, he saw the scissors in her hands, but couldn't stop the forward motion of his body. The blades punctured his chest and then darkness.

Annalise heard the gasp of the person holding the scissors before she pushed Benjamin away and he crumpled to the floor. The scene jumped to the killer deleting the photos on the camera. When she reached the last of the photos, she walked back to place the camera in its bag on the luggage rack where she'd found it when Benjamin went into the bathroom. She dropped the scissors which she'd wrapped in a hand towel from the bathroom into her purse along with the memory card.

Annalise opened her eyes. Now she knew how Benjamin had been killed. Her phone rang and she jumped, startled by the sharpness of the sound in the quiet of her room. *Let it go to voice mail. You need to pull yourself together,* was her first thought, but when she saw Liam's name on the screen, she answered.

"I promised myself I'd wait at least four days, maybe five, before I called again so I wouldn't be making a pest of myself, but I couldn't do it. I hope you don't mind."

Liam's voice had a settling effect on her and her lips curved up in a soft smile.

"It was perfect timing."

"If you don't have plans, would it be okay if I came over tonight?" he asked.

"How about I come to your house instead? I was just thinking I needed to get out of the house for a bit, and someone in the Universe must have been listening, because that's when you called." She started to say more about the vision she'd had, but stopped. *It's too soon to tell him that you're psychic. You don't want to scare him off.*

"That's me, your knight in shining armor."

She felt his smile and her body relaxed. She sent a silent thank you to the Universe.

"What time should I be there?"

"Is six too early? We could have some appetizers and I have a bottle of wine in the fridge."

"That works."

"Alright, I'll see you then."

"Liam..." she caught him before he hung up. "I don't know where you live."

There was silence on the line, but she knew he was still there. "Right," he said at last. "I completely forgot you haven't been here yet. It feels like we've been together a lot longer than we have. In a good way," he rushed on.

Annalise laughed softly. "I feel the same way."

He gave her the information, which she typed into her Contacts. When she entered his address into her Maps app, she realized she'd driven by his Cape Cod-style house many times, but hadn't known it was his. He didn't have a sign for his shop, but since he didn't use it as a place to sell his pottery, there was no need for one.

His call was exactly what she needed to lift herself out of the funk her vision had put her in. She'd let the ladies know what she'd seen, but not tonight.

————

She arrived at his house, decorated with a string of icicle lights across the roofline on the front side. It was the one touch of holiday decorations. *No blow-up snow men or reindeer, not that I was expecting any,* but for reasons she couldn't articulate, that pleased her. She arrived on time, despite having gone through three wardrobe changes before deciding on red wide-legged slacks and a bright, to the point of garish, multi-colored floral silk blouse that draped loosely around her body. Her fashion style leaned toward Bohemian and the blouse reflected that aesthetic.

She rang the doorbell and her eyes got wide as saucers and her jaw dropped when instead of a traditional chime, she heard *"I command you, in the name of the Knights of Camelot, to open the door of this sacred castle."* She dissolved into a fit of laughter and was unable to stop before Liam opened the door.

She wiped tears from her eyes and walked into the foyer, still chuckling, but more in control.

"I take it you're a Monty Python fan," she said.

At first he pretended not to know what she meant, but couldn't keep up the pretense.

"You must be a fan, too, if you got the reference."

"We'll have to have a contest sometime to see who can remember the most iconic lines from their skits."

"You're on," he said. "I knew there was a reason I like you."

The foyer was small, with a stairway leading up to the second story slightly to the left of the center of the house. A hallway to its right led into the kitchen. Liam took her coat and hung it in the closet while Annalise waited. Her eyes were drawn to the right where the living room was located. He had a fire going in the fireplace and she spotted the stocking he'd bought from her hanging on the mantel. Liam followed her eyes to the stocking.

"It looks like it was made for that spot, doesn't it?"

"Yes, it does. Do you think Santa will leave you something nice or a lump of coal?"

"It will definitely be something nice, but since Santa won't be the one filling it, I will, that's not much of a gamble. Why don't you sit down and I'll bring in the appetizers and wine?"

Two couches were placed facing each other on either side of the fireplace with a coffee table in between. She chose the one that gave her a view of the dining room adjacent to the living room. Decorating the mantle and coffee table were pottery pieces she recognized as ones he made. As she took another look around the room, its simple lines and muted tones made her think of a page right out of a Pottery Barn catalogue, and she stifled a laugh. She wondered if he was aware of the cliché of a potter using that décor.

Liam returned carrying a tray with the wine, two plates, glasses, and a charcuterie board. He set it down on the table, poured a glass for each of them, and handed her one before sitting on the other end of the couch facing her.

"How do you like the charcuterie board? I bought it from Quentin."

She looked closer. Liam had filled the board with so much food that only half an inch of the edges was visible.

"What I can see of it is beautiful."

"Good point. We'll just have to start eating so we can see more of it. Dig in," Liam said, handing her a plate. "Tell me what you've been up to the past few days."

"I've been playing catch up with clients and cleaning my sewing room. I went to lunch with Eva and Jennifer and Penelope Butler joined us."

"She's the weaver?"

"That's right. She had a lot to say about the craft fair shenanigans," Annalise said.

"Did you really say shenanigans?" he teased.

"It's a perfectly good word," she said, affecting that she'd been insulted, even though she wasn't. "She has a theory that Violet is behind at least some of it." Annalise wanted to hear his perspective. Everything the Club had learned pointed toward Violet, but she needed someone's opinion who could be objective.

"Interesting. I haven't been living here long so I don't have the history that most of you do, but I don't find that unbelievable. It's in her eyes. Her words come out friendly enough, but there's a coldness in her eyes."

"You're right about a history. I grew up with several of the vendors and Violet was always jealous of them. She's actually a talented artist but never on the same level as Sophia. Penny told us Bethany turned Violet down to have a table because she'd already told Sophia she could have the spot and wanted to have a mix of crafts. She probably shouldn't have let us in because Abigail is a quilter, but her quilts are on a different level than ours and she doesn't make the smaller things like we do."

"Penny thinks Violet slashed the painting and stole Fiona's things?"

"She doesn't know that for a fact, but she thinks it could be possible. And we, the other Club ladies and I, think she's responsible for Willow's peanut reaction." She told him about their visit with Nathan.

He shook his head in amazement. "I've never lived in a town this small before. I thought it was all a stereotype for TV and the movies about small towns being all rainbows and unicorns on the outside with everyone helping each other out, but hiding a dark underbelly. Over the past couple of weeks, I've begun to rethink that."

"I've lived here all my life so I don't have a frame of reference for how things are in other small towns, but Glen Lake does have some of what you described. I think the balance leans toward the rainbows and unicorns, though. I hope recent events aren't making you reconsider staying here."

"No. Even if it is a hotbed of iniquity, I can hide out in my pottery studio and see what and whoever I want to. Meeting you and the other quilt club gals and Jim have made me realize there are some good reasons for sticking my head out every so often, though."

"I'm glad to hear it." She considered feeling him out about his theories regarding Benjamin's death, but she'd come here to escape that negativity. "And in that spirit of positivity, let's talk about more pleasant things, like your penchant for décor a la Pottery Barn."

CHAPTER 27

"It seems strange to all be here together without our ugly sweaters and sitting at your table. I think this is the first time we've all been together since the craft fair," Sarah said.

They were gathered at Eva's house for an afternoon Christmas party instead of their regular meeting and potluck. Twelve bags of cookies were the night's centerpiece. Each of them had brought three bags filled with a dozen cookies which they would swap and take home.

"This was such a great idea, Eva. Dave and the kids have been disappointed that I hadn't made any Christmas cookies, but it's been too hectic. When I explained to them that they couldn't have any of the ones I was baking today, but I'd have three dozen when I got home, that made them happy. I sort of forgot to tell them that the other dozen from this batch were hidden in the pantry," Jennifer said, rolling her eyes.

"You aren't hoarding them all for yourself, are you?" Eva asked.

"No, not that I wasn't tempted. I'll put them all in the cookie jar and they'll never be the wiser that they could have had them sooner."

"You are a mean and devious woman," Annalise teased.

"It comes with years of experience," Jennifer said, winking.

"Phil called earlier to tell me that he and Dennis went to the hotel to check the security tapes," Sarah said. She reached out for one of the bags, removed a cookie, and began munching on it. "What?" Three pairs of eyes were staring at her. "I only took my share," she said, smiling broadly, unaffected by the gawks she was getting.

"Oh, what the heck," Annalise said, and took a bag for herself. "I love peanut butter blossoms. These are really delicious," she said to Jennifer through a mouthful of cookie.

Eva and Jennifer exchanged looks and shrugged their shoulders.

"Might as well join the crowd," Eva said, taking one of her cookie goodie bags. "You were telling us about Phil and Dennis," she reminded Sarah.

"Before I was so rudely interrupted." She feigned annoyance but they all smiled. "They think they have Violet on the security tape walking through the lobby and going up in the elevators." She told them the details of what they'd seen on the security tapes and heard from Tim Wright after showing him the photo. "It's still not enough to bring her in because her face isn't visible. They're checking the car registration to see if it's hers."

"I missed the part about why they think it was Violet if they couldn't see her face," Jennifer said.

"She was wearing the same outfit as she had on in one of the photos from the craft fair. Obviously, it's not custom-made so she could claim that anyone who shops at the store where she bought hers could have the same one. That's all they've got."

"My turn," Annalise said. "Yesterday afternoon I was cleaning up my sewing room and I must have been channeling you, Jennifer. When I picked up my scissors, I had the thought pop into my head that Benjamin was killed with scissors. I went to my sitting room and did a meditation just in case I could get more information. I didn't see pictures right away like you do, but maybe this was different because the scissors belonged to me."

"This happened yesterday afternoon?" Eva asked when Annalise finished telling them about her vision.

Annalise nodded, her mouth full of another bite of her cookie.

"So why are we just hearing about this now? And have you talked to Phil and Dennis?"

Annalise's hand stopped midway to her mouth before she could take another bite and her cheeks turned pink. She stalled by taking a sip of her tea. *Just spit it out, Annalise. These are your friends. They're not going to judge you.*

"I totally get what you were feeling. It can be unnerving having those images in your head coming at you, especially when you're not expecting them," Jennifer said, almost as though she'd read Annalise's mind.

"Thanks, Jen. Right after the vision ended, I got a call from Liam and he invited me to come to his house. Well, technically, I invited myself but it was only because I needed to get out. He'd asked if he could come to see me, but…" She stopped, aware that she'd been rattling out the words.

"You don't have to be self-conscious about that, Lise," Eva said, covering Annalise's hand with her own.

Annalise took a deep breath. "I know. You'd think I was a teenager again and my mom caught me sneaking out my bedroom window to meet my boyfriend. Not that that ever happened, of course," she said, rolling her eyes.

"So, have you told Phil and Dennis?" Sarah brought the question back around.

"Not yet. I should have called them but I couldn't see Violet's face to be sure it really was her, so I didn't think it was urgent. And I guess I wanted to talk it over with all of you to get your opinions."

"You should call them first thing tomorrow," Eva said. "If it really was her and those were her scissors, that could narrow down what they'll need to look for when it gets to be time for a search warrant."

"I promise. First thing tomorrow. Cross my heart," she said as she made the motion with the index and middle finger of her right hand.

CHAPTER 28

"Hi, Dennis. This is Annalise Jordan. It may be nothing, but I promised Eva I'd call you this morning about a vision I had a couple nights ago regarding Benjamin Brooks's murder."

"Has Sarah filled you in about our person of interest?" he asked.

"Yes. We all agree that's the right person to be investigating. This is about the murder weapon."

"Oh? You have a theory?"

Annalise was glad they weren't Face Timing so he couldn't see her smile at his use of the word theory instead of vision. She understood.

"Yes. My theory is that the murder weapon is a pair of scissors. Benjamin had been drugged so he was unsteady on his feet. I'll stop here to clarify that I haven't seen the killer's face in any of my visions. Anyway, the person with Benjamin heard him coming out of the bathroom and that's when she took the scissors out of her purse. I don't think she intended to hurt him. She had them to defend herself if he attacked. Which he didn't, but because she had drugged him, he lost his balance and fell toward her and she couldn't move out of the way in time. She took a hand towel from the bathroom to wipe off the scissors and her gloves and then wrapped them in the towel. She took it with her along with the memory card, after she'd used the camera to delete some of the photos."

"Why did she bother taking the memory card, then, if she'd deleted the photos?"

"I got the impression it had been her intent to do that from the start. I asked Sarah the same question and she told me about using the camera and said it would be easier that way. It doesn't make sense to me either, though, why she wanted the card if the pictures weren't on it anymore."

"Do you know where she put the scissors and her gloves?"

"I'm sorry, no. It wasn't part of the vision. That's why I didn't call you earlier but Eva thought I should tell you anyway, and you could do with it whatever you want."

"Well, it's nothing we can use to get a search warrant," Dennis said, drily.

"Of course, not," Annalise said, bristling. She'd thought they knew her better by now than to be so dismissive of information she received through her visions.

"I'm sorry. That didn't come out the way I meant it. It really wasn't meant to be personal. You've never steered us wrong before."

His apology took away her defensiveness. "Thank you for saying that. It hasn't been easy to put myself out like this to people in your position. I wouldn't waste your time if I didn't think it might help."

"It always has, and I'm confident it will this time, too. I was just frustrated that we have so much circumstantial evidence but nothing strong enough to take it to that next step."

"I understand. I don't think you'll have to wait much longer, though. You're getting close," Annalise reassured him.

"I believe you. In the meantime, I'm going to talk this over with Phil and figure out where we go from here. Thanks, Annalise. I mean that."

Phil walked into the office they shared as Dennis was hanging up.

"We have a new lead on the Brooks case."

"Oh?" Phil said. His eyes reflected the curiosity in his voice.

"That was Annalise Jordan. She had a vision about the murder weapon."

CHAPTER 29

"What if we interview her anyway?" Phil asked once Dennis had filled him in. "We can tell her we're interviewing all of the vendors and volunteers from the craft fair."

Dennis nodded his head. "Yeah, that's not a bad idea. It might make her nervous enough to slip up. Should we mention the hotel?"

"I think so. Let's see how far we can push her if we show her pictures from the security cameras. We've got the screen grabs in the file and her address from her license and car registration."

"Okay, let's do this."

———

"Looks like we got lucky. Her car's in the driveway," Phil said when they arrived at Violet's small, but well-maintained ranch-style home. The yard was decorated with a four-foot tall creche and nativity scene. Lights, unlit now, were strung around the evergreen shrubs and along the roofline. A wooden welcome sign with a snowman painted on it was hung beside the door and the door itself was decorated with a live evergreen wreath.

"I'm going to feel a little like the Grinch stealing Christmas when we arrest her," Phil said, looking around at the festive displays.

"At least she's having a Christmas. Benjamin Brooks won't ever be enjoying one again," Dennis reminded him.

They didn't have long to wait for Violet to answer the doorbell.

"Can I help you?" She eyed them both suspiciously as she stood with one hand on the open door as though she was preparing to close it if she didn't like their reply.

"Good morning, Ms. Ouellette. May we come in? We have some questions about Benjamin Brooks," Phil said after they'd identified themselves and shown Violet their badges.

"I don't know what I could tell you," she said, standing her ground and not asking them to come in.

"We're interviewing all of the vendors and volunteers from the craft fair in case they saw or heard anything that can help. You might have seen something that didn't seem out of the ordinary at the time, but might be important," Dennis replied.

She gave them each a hard stare before begrudgingly standing aside so they could enter. The interior of the house was tastefully decorated with paintings that were original pieces, not off the shelf box store décor.

"You have a lovely home. Did you do the artwork? It's very good," Phil said, hoping to loosen her up.

It worked. Violet's entire demeanor changed and her chest puffed up with pride.

"Why, thank you. Yes, I'm the artist." She graced him with a smile.

"You're very talented," Dennis added for good measure.

"Thank you. Have a seat," she gestured toward the living room.

They chose the chairs positioned on either side of the couch with the coffee table between them. Dennis laid the unopened folder with the photos on the table. Violet sat on the couch and waited for them to begin.

"It's our understanding that you were a volunteer, not a vendor. Is that correct?" Phil asked.

She drew her lips into a tight line and sat rigidly with her hands folded in her lap. She didn't answer immediately and it appeared as though she was considering how to reply.

"Yes, she said, at last. "I asked to be given a table, but Bethany Cox told me I couldn't have one."

"Why was that?" Phil asked.

"You'd have to ask her," Violet replied, stiffly.

"We'll do that," Dennis said. "We've been told there were some incidents at the fair." He took his notebook from his jacket pocket and flipped to the page he wanted. "Fiona Walsh said she had some items stolen and one of Sophia Peterson's paintings was slashed." He looked up from his notebook and met her eyes.

"Yes, I'm aware of that. I don't know anything about Fiona's things, but Sophia's painting was torn because she had a rough edge on her easel. I showed her that the day it happened. Is she still claiming someone did it on purpose?"

"She seems to think it was suspicious. Her easel hadn't been damaged before the day it happened. We thought you might have seen someone around her table when she wasn't looking?"

"No. I told you. She caused a stink about it and tried to blame Miles Clarke. She's always been jealous of him," she added as an aside. "Anyway, I was standing there with some of the attendees when Sophia had her tantrum. I even cut my finger on the rough spot on the easel when I picked up the painting. She's making something out of nothing." Violet sat primly with her hands folded on her lap and waited for their next question, since obviously nothing more needed to be said about the matter of the painting.

"Can you tell us anything about the incident with Willow Stone?" Phil asked.

"Nathan had peanuts at his table. When he opened the package, she had an allergic reaction."

"He told us you had given him the peanuts," Phil pressed on.

Violet clenched her hands, turning the knuckles white. "Well, yes. He told me he was hungry when I went to his table to ask if he needed anything. Neither of us knew Willow was allergic," her chin tilted up defensively. "I don't see what anything of this has to do with Benjamin Brooks."

"You know, of course, that he was there because he was working on a book. He took a lot of photos from what we understand. His memory card was missing from his camera when his hotel room was searched, but then it turned up at the fair. It seems logical that the two are connected," Dennis said.

"Wasn't it found at Quentin Gray's table? Did anyone tell you they'd had a feud from years ago?"

"We have been told about that. We were also told that you'd been spreading that story around."

"I was just repeating what other people had been talking about," she sniffed. Her mouth had returned to its tight-lipped position and her eyes had turned cold. Her hands clenched together even tighter. "Did you ask him about it?" she demanded.

"We did. He told us that was years ago and not something he'd kill anyone over. He also had an airtight alibi for the night of the murder."

"Oh," she said, deflating slightly.

Dennis picked up the folder and pulled out the photo of Violet walking through the lobby.

"Do you recognize this person?" he asked, handing her the photo.

Her eyes flickered and the color drained from her cheeks.

"No, should I?" she said, handing him back the photo and leveling her eyes with his.

"We believe she is the person who murdered Mr. Brooks." He put the photo back in the file and removed the photos taken at the rear entrance and of her getting into her car. "How about these photos? Maybe there's something about the way she's dressed or her posture that seems familiar."

She took the photos, glanced at them, and handed them back.

"Again, why would I recognize this person? I can't even see her face. And what makes you think I would have seen her before?"

"We thought she might have been at the fair. As we said, we believe there's a connection," Dennis continued.

"The car in the parking lot looks a lot like yours," Phil interjected.

Her head whipped in his direction.

"It's a very popular model. There must be hundreds of them in the area. Does the license plate number match mine?" She'd studied the photo long enough to figure out the number wasn't legible, and they couldn't prove it was hers.

"Our techs are working on cleaning up the photo. We don't have the number yet, but we should soon," he bluffed.

"Did you talk to Bethany Cox? I heard them arguing in the lobby and she told him she wouldn't let him get away with it. I don't know what the "it" was about. They stopped talking as soon as they saw me."

"We are aware of that. We haven't been able to talk to her yet. But we will," Phil said.

"Would it be possible to use your bathroom?" Dennis asked, making both Phil and Violet look at him in bewilderment.

"Um, of course. It's the second door on the right in the hallway. I'll show you," she started to stand up.

"No need. I can find it."

Phil and Violet sat in an awkward silence until he returned minutes later.

"I don't have any other questions. Do you?" he asked Dennis.

"No, I think we're done."

"Thank you for your time, Ms. Ouellette," Phil said, extending his hand for her to shake. Dennis did the same. "If you do think of anything or can identify the woman in the photos, please let us know." They each handed her their card and she walked them to the door.

"I think we got to her," Dennis said as they pulled out of her driveway and headed back to the station.

"That's what I think, too," Phil said. "But we've still got to prove it's her," his tone less optimistic than Dennis's.

"What was that about with the bathroom?" Phil asked.

"I did a medicine cabinet check. It's not admissible in court, but I found a bottle of sleeping pills. I'm pretty sure they'll match the ones that turned up in Brooks's autopsy report."

————

Violet watched through the slit she'd created by pulling back the curtain at the living room window as they backed out of the driveway.

They think it's me. Somehow they suspect it's me.

Her heart was racing and her breathing became rapid and shallow. She closed her eyes and forced herself to take slow breaths in and out to avoid the looming full-blown panic attack.

CHAPTER 30

The fire in the wood stove had finally taken the chill off the room, but Violet remained wrapped in the wool blanket, hypnotized by the flames. She'd escaped to her cabin on the lake. She'd had to get away from the house to think... and plan. Along with the firewood she'd used to start the fire, she'd thrown in the dress and hat she'd worn to the hotel. There wasn't anything she could do about the car, but she was almost positive they were bluffing about being able to read the license plate.

I can't stay here too long. If I go missing, that will give them even more reason to suspect I did it. Just a day or two, maybe three, to clear my head.

They already suspect you did it.

But they can't prove it. They don't have the murder weapon. They might not know it was scissors that killed him and even if they do, I bleached them and the gloves. There won't be any DNA they can test on them.

I should have gotten rid of them.

No, that would make you look guilty, too. If they search the house, it would be more suspicious if you didn't still have them.

There's no way they can prove it was you. They were fishing with the photos. And now they won't find the clothes. She smiled as she watched them burning.

I should call Nathan. Find out what he told them. I might have gone too far with the peanuts. That was a mistake. I just wanted to get back at Marylou and if I couldn't pay her back, Willow was the next best thing.

She took out her phone and searched through the contacts until she found his number.

"Nathan," she said in her cheeriest voice. "Have you recovered from the craft fair?"

She only half-listened to him talk. She needed to find out about the peanuts.

"I had a visit from the detectives investigating Benjamin's murder. They said they'd talked to you, too," she said once he'd finally wound down.

"Yes, they wanted to know if I'd seen or heard anyone threatening him, which I didn't. They asked about Willow's reaction to the peanuts, too, which I thought was odd. Annalise Jordan had asked me about them, too."

"Annalise Jordan?" Violet's spidey senses started to tingle.

"Yes, she and Jennifer and Eva came to my shop to do some Christmas shopping and we were talking about the fair. Annalise asked me if I knew Willow had a peanut allergy. Of course, I said I didn't or I never would have been eating them. She asked me where I got them and I told her you'd given them to me."

"Okay. I've got to go, Nathan. Someone's at the door."

No one was at the door but it was the best excuse she could think of to end the call.

Annalise Jordan. I never liked Annalise. She thought she was better than everyone else. And here she is causing trouble for me again after all these years.

They'd managed to mostly stay out of each other's way in the decades since high school. The craft fair was the first time they'd spent that much time in each other's company.

I might have to pay Ms. Jordan a visit. See what she told the cops.

It wasn't much of a plan, but she had a direction.

Just keep cool and stick to your story. They can't prove anything.

She put another log on the fire and snuggled back up in her blanket. Her head began to nod, so she stretched out on the couch, and relaxed now, she slept.

CHAPTER 31

"'m glad we finally caught up with each other, Mrs. Cox," Phil said. He and Dennis were in their office at the police station. They'd been playing telephone tag with Bethany for days.

"Yes, it's been a whirlwind here with my husband's heart attack."

"I'm sorry to hear that. Is he okay now?"

"Yes, they kept him overnight, but it was a mild attack. He isn't happy about having to change his diet and start exercising, but the doctors told him if he didn't, he might not be as fortunate if he has another one."

"Good luck. I hope you can keep him healthy."

"Oh, I've already started. He was even less happy when he looked in the pantry and refrigerator and discovered I'd cleaned out all the unhealthy snacks. And to add a little more salt to the wound, I signed us both up for a gym membership. I figured I could use the exercise, too, and when I go, he'll go."

Phil chuckled. "He doesn't realize how lucky he is to have you on his team."

"He can be a pain at times, but I love him, and I want him to be around for a long time. Now, I understand you want to ask me about the craft fair and Benjamin Brooks."

"That's right. Two witnesses observed you arguing with him in the lobby and heard you make a threatening remark. Can you tell me about that?"

"Oh, that. I was worried because I'd seen him taking pictures when Sophia Peterson was having her meltdown about her painting getting torn. I was afraid he would try to spin it to make us look bad. I'd heard about what he'd done to Quentin Gray and didn't want it happening to us. This was our first year for the craft fair and we're hoping to make it an annual event. We raised a lot of money for the summer youth programs. He called me later and asked if I could meet him at his hotel so he could show me pictures he'd taken. He thought I would want to see them because he'd caught someone slashing the painting, just like Sophia said. I asked him to just tell me who it was and I'd take care of it, but he said I should look at the pictures first. He never got the chance to do that. We were supposed to meet the morning after he was killed. I called his cell phone that morning to reschedule, but didn't get an answer so I called the front desk. The clerk probably shouldn't have, but he told me he couldn't leave a message for him because Benjamin had been killed."

"I'm sorry, but I have to ask you where you were the night he died," Phil said.

"That's the night my husband had his heart attack. We were in the ER most of the night. Natalie Johnson can vouch for me. She was on duty that night. I can give you her number," Bethany offered.

"Thank you, but we already have it. We were the detectives assigned to the Caleb Mitchell murder."

"Ohh," Bethany said, understanding the reference. The month before Natalie Johnson's husband had been a suspect in the murder of his law partner, Caleb Mitchell. It made sense to her that the detectives would have had contact with Natalie as part of the investigation.

"What about the accusation that someone stole items belonging to Fiona Walsh?"

"We never found out who took them or how it happened. Fiona swears up and down that they were in her tote when she left the night before and missing the next day. There aren't any security cameras in the cafeteria but the school is locked. The only ones who had permission to unlock it were Violet Ouellette and myself."

"Who was the first one in on the morning Fiona reported the theft?" Phil asked.

"I was running a little late, so Violet opened up for me," Bethany said. "But I can't imagine she would have taken them. Why would she? Especially knowing it would point the finger at her because of the timing. I did ask her about it and she wasn't very happy with me, but she said she didn't do it. She figured Fiona either miscounted or she'd sold them earlier and forgot to write the sales down. That seemed logical to me. It had been a busy day and she was by herself. It would have been very easy to get interrupted with the next customer and forget to record the sale."

"Did anything seem odd to you about the incident with Willow Stone?"

"No, that was an accident. Nathan didn't know about her allergy. I should take some of the blame for that because I forgot to tell the vendors. Thank goodness she had her Epi pen and it all turned out fine."

"Was Violet Ouellette aware of the allergy?" Phil asked.

"I think she was. It was on Willow's vendor application form and I believe she looked through them, but we never talked about it specifically. It's my fault, though, for not telling the vendors. That was supposed to be my task."

"Did you know that Violet gave Nathan the peanuts?"

"She *what*? I didn't know that." Bethany's voice trailed off as the implications of Violet's actions sunk in. "I suppose it's possible she hadn't read the forms, after all," she added, not willing to accept Violet may have done it on purpose.

"I think that covers all the questions I had. If you think of anything else or if you remember any unusual interactions Mr. Brooks may have had either with vendors or attendees at the fair, you have my number."

Phil turned to Dennis when he'd disconnected the call. "She has an alibi for the night of the murder. I'm going to call Natalie Johnson to confirm it."

"Was that who you were talking about when you mentioned Caleb Mitchell?" Dennis asked.

"Yes. Natalie was on duty in the ER when Bethany Cox's husband was having a heart attack. Bethany told me that's where she was when Brooks was murdered. Her husband was admitted and was there overnight. It's just a formality to check since we're 99.9 percent sure it was Violet Ouellette, but better to cross the t's and dot the i's."

"Seems like that's all the progress, if you can call it that, that we've made," Dennis said and sighed. "She's the only one we haven't been able to eliminate, but we can't prove it's her, either. Where do we go from here?"

Phil shrugged. "Maybe the Quilts Club ladies will learn something new. They've saved our cases before."

"Should we call the ghostbusters?" Dennis joked.

"Not the worst piece of advice I've had today," Phil said. "You should probably close the door. We don't want to take a chance that someone overhears us."

CHAPTER 32

"Did you arrest her?" Sarah asked as soon as she answered Dennis's call.

"Sad to say, not yet." He stalled before continuing with the reason for the call. "I've got you on speaker. Phil and I were just talking about how you ladies have helped us out and we thought maybe…" He waited for her to pick up the thread.

"Since you're calling me, it's either about hacking an account or talking to Benjamin," she obliged him.

"Yeah," he said, and she heard the contriteness in his voice. "If we could get you into the hotel room, do you think you could ask him some questions for us? Or maybe he'd tell you himself who killed him," he said, hopefully.

"How soon do you want to do this? I'm out straight today, but have time tomorrow or the next day."

Dennis exhaled as though he'd been holding his breath. "That's great! We'll have to run it by the hotel anyway, but I'll try for tomorrow. Sooner is better than later. I'll text you when I have a day and time."

"Should I be feeling ashamed of myself?" he asked Phil, after disconnecting his call with Sarah.

"Maybe, but so should I," Phil answered.

"Then how come I don't?"

Phil just shrugged.

"And don't forget, you're going to be there for this one!" Dennis said.

Only Dennis had been with Sarah when she connected with Caleb Mitchell's spirit the month before. It was the first time either detective had witnessed her in action, but afterwards Dennis informed Phil that he would have to be there the next time.

"I ain't afraid of no ghost," Phil replied, glibly.

"Then you've never been around one," Dennis growled. "Tell me that after you've seen Sarah talk to Brooks."

Sarah picked up her phone when the text notification alert pinged.

DENNIS

> The hotel will let us in the room tomorrow at nine AM. The room is booked later that day, so we'll have to be out before three PM. Don't imagine it should take that long, though.

> Not if he's there and ready to talk. I'll meet you in the lobby.

DENNIS

CHAPTER 33

Harper Hughes wasn't there, but the manager-on-duty that day opened the door to the room where Brooks had been staying and let them inside.

"I had Housekeeping clean the room early so you won't be disturbed," he told them, but made no move to leave.

"We can take it from here," Phil told him.

The manager took the hint and left. He didn't speak, but the disappointed look he gave them said it all.

"Dennis told me what happened when you talked to Caleb Mitchell, but how does this work? Can I say anything while you're talking to Brooks? Like if I think of something I want you to ask him? Dennis said he couldn't actually hear what Caleb was saying but you told him and Dylan what was going on."

Sarah smiled as Phil asked his questions. She explained her process as he nodded, taking it in.

"You two can sit there," she said pointing to the table and chairs near the window. "I'm going to look around in the bathroom first, and if I don't sense anything, I'll come back out. I'm not picking up anything yet in this area, but he may need a minute to let me know he's here." She started to walk toward the bathroom and then stopped abruptly. "This is where his body was found, isn't it?"

Phil looked at Dennis, his eyes big as saucers. Dennis gave him an *I told you so* smug smile.

"Yes. That's right where they found him."

She nodded and walked into the bathroom, but returned in less than a minute. She walked back to the exit door, turned around, and walked slowly back into the main part of the room. She stopped at the spot where she'd sensed his body had been found. Remembering what Annalise had told her about her vision of the murder, she stepped back to where the killer would have been standing and waited. She shivered almost imperceptibly but both Dennis and Phil had seen it. And then they felt the cold, too.

"It's Sarah Pascal, Benjamin. We met at the Glen Lake craft fair. I was with the Cozy Quilts Club ladies."

She paused, waiting for him to acknowledge her.

"I remember, but why are you here with the detectives?"

"We think we know who your killer was but can't prove it yet. Can you tell us what happened and did you know the killer?"

Benjamin repeated what Annalise had seen, with the exception that he named Violet as his killer.

"Thank you. We thought it was Violet, but needed your confirmation," she said more for Phil and Dennis's benefit than Benjamin's. "Can you tell us what she used for a weapon?"

"It was a pair of scissors. She wasn't facing me when I came out of the bathroom but I could see she had my camera. When she heard me, she started fumbling around in her purse and then pulled something out. I couldn't tell what it was but I wanted to know what she was doing with my camera. I just wanted to take it away from her but she stuck out her hand when I got closer. That's when I figured out it was a pair of scissors but I was so sleepy and I couldn't keep my balance, and then I fell…"

Sarah was overcome with a sensation of grief and knew she would have to move on and divert Benjamin's attention or she might lose their connection.

"Why was Violet here?"

"I saw her cut Sophia's painting. She didn't know that I was watching her and taking her picture. When I confronted her and she didn't confess to doing it, I hung around after the fair was over so I could talk to her alone. When I said I had proof, she still didn't believe me, so I invited her to come to the hotel and I would show her the pictures. I had a zoom meeting with my publisher so I didn't have time to do it then. And I wanted to upload them to my cloud account before the meeting in case my editor wanted to look at any of them."

"I was able to access your cloud account, Benjamin. We found the photos Violet deleted but there weren't any photos of her slashing the painting."

"I put those photos in a separate file and encrypted it. It wasn't named anything you'd associate with the craft fair. I didn't want my editor to see them by accident."

"Would you give me the name of the file so I can find those photos? We don't have anything yet that ties her to any crimes at the fair. We might be able to use them to get her to confess." She turned to Phil. "Phil, would you please hand me that pad of paper and the pen."

Benjamin gave her the file name and the password to unlock it and she wrote it down. Something else occurred to her.

"Benjamin, were you trying to blackmail Violet?"

"No. I was hoping she would realize it would be better to confess and make amends to Sophia on her own. I had no idea she would react like she did. It wasn't like she would go to jail if it got out. At worst, it would be a charge of vandalism."

"From what I've learned about Violet, I think it had more to do with her reputation. She's never felt like she was good enough and wasn't accepted on the same terms as the other artists at the fair. I don't know that for sure, of course, but if I had to guess, that's what I think she had on her mind. She only wanted to delete the photos from your camera so you couldn't show them to Bethany or Sophia. You would be moving on once the fair was over, but she lives here."

"Yes. I don't think she meant to kill me. I saw the expression on her face when I fell. The scissors were in her hand and she didn't have time to move away. It happened too quickly. She expected the sleeping pills to kick in so she could get to my camera, but she underestimated how long it would take."

Sarah recapped their conversation for the detectives. "Is there anything you want to ask him?"

"I can't think of anything. Can you?" Phil asked Dennis. He shook his head.

"Thank you, Benjamin. This has been helpful. I'll check your cloud account as soon as I'm back at my computer. It won't prove that Violet killed you, but it could help to build the case for a motive."

She waited until his image had faded before she informed the detectives they were done.

"If you have time, why don't you follow me home and I'll access the file now?"

Once they were all back at Sarah's office and she had logged into Benjamin's account, she took out the information he had given her and found the file. Just as he'd told her, there were five photos of Violet standing in front of the painting. In one, she was looking around the room as though she was making sure no one was watching, but either didn't notice him or thought he was too far away to see what she was doing. What she didn't have any way of knowing was that the lens on his camera was able to catch her moves even from that distance. He snapped photos as she unsheathed a small knife she'd taken from her purse and palmed it in her hand. She leaned into the painting and raised her hand with the knife up to it. For anyone who might be watching, it would give the impression that she was examining the brush strokes. She slid her hand down the painting only an inch or two and smiled. She reached back with the knife still in her palm and dropped it into her open purse at the same time that she took hold of the purse's strap. She was still smiling as she walked away.

CHAPTER 34

Sarah printed the photos for the detectives to take with them.

"I'm not optimistic this will break her. She came across as being someone who would stick to their story if they thought they could get away with it, but thanks, Sarah," Dennis said.

"Sure. Keep me posted."

"Absolutely," Phil promised.

"The pictures might be enough to rattle her. I think we should give it another try tomorrow. You've got court this afternoon," Dennis reminded Phil when they were back in their car. He glanced over at Phil who was staring out the passenger window and hadn't appeared to have heard him.

"Earth to Phil," he said, raising his voice to make sure he got through.

"Huh? What?" Phil said, looking over at Dennis. He had a distant look in his eyes.

"You didn't hear a word I just said, did you? Are you thinking about what happened at the hotel?"

"Yeah. A part of me still doesn't want to believe it happened. And you don't have to remind me that we've taken her word for it before and you've already been through this with the Mitchell case. Is this how you felt, too?"

"Pretty much. It doesn't help that we can't hear the other side of the conversation, but she tells us information we didn't have and it all turns out to be true."

"She could have known about the other file, but just didn't tell us," Phil's skeptical side argued.

Dennis nodded. "That's a fair point, but I don't think Sarah would do that. Do you?"

"No," Phil said, although somewhat begrudgingly.

"This is part of the reason I wanted you to be there. I don't think this will be the last case we work with them and they haven't steered us wrong so far. If nothing else, it's a sign of respect that we believe them."

It was Phil's turn to nod. He let out a deep breath, an external sign of his subconscious letting go of the resistance he'd been holding onto.

"As I was saying before. You've got to be in court this afternoon, but I think we should go back to Violet Ouellette's house tomorrow and show her these photos."

"It might be enough to rattle her," Phil said.

Dennis gave him a side eye. "That's what I just said. You really weren't listening, were you?"

Phil knew the question was rhetorical.

CHAPTER 35

Dennis knocked on the door again; a little louder this time, when Violet hadn't responded. Her car wasn't in the driveway but it could have been inside the garage. An elderly woman in the neighboring house opened her door, an oversized sweater wrapped around her. She remained in the doorway peering at them over the frame of her eyeglasses which had slid down on her nose.

"She's not home." Her voice was strong in contrast to her stooped shoulders and frail body.

Phil and Dennis turned their heads toward her and, once she knew she had their attention, she continued.

"She took off a few days ago. Had a suitcase so she must be planning to be away for a while."

"Thanks, ma'am. Do you have any idea where she might have gone?" Dennis asked.

She gave him a disgusted look. "How should I know? I'm not her secretary." She went back inside shutting the door hard enough for them to hear it, but not quite a slam.

Phil and Dennis looked at each other, their eyebrows raised.

"Might as well go back to the station. We're not going to get anywhere today," Phil said.

"Do you think she's on the run?" Dennis asked.

"It's a possibility."

"Should we call and leave a voice mail?"

Phil thought this over. "No. If she really is on the run, it won't make her come back. She might have already had plans to go somewhere and this is only a coincidence. Giving her the benefit of the doubt here."

"Maybe we should ask Annalise." Dennis was only half-joking.

"Give her a call," Phil replied, much to Dennis's surprise, but he took out his phone. "It's going to voice mail."

"Leave her a message but keep it vague in case anyone else hears it. Just say we're trying to find Violet and we thought she might know where she is."

"I hope she can read between the lines," Dennis said after he disconnected.

CHAPTER 36

nnalise listened to the voice mail for a second time, and it came to her what Dennis was really asking. She'd only been half-listening the first time and thought she must have missed some vital piece of information.

"Violet's gone missing," she said aloud to the empty room. Her next client wouldn't be coming for another two hours. Time enough for her to try a meditation. She went to her sitting room and began her ritual. She picked a CD and placed it in the player, lit a scented candle, and sat in her chair. She slowed her breathing and unfocused her eyes, concentrating her thoughts on Violet until, like watching a scene in a movie, images appeared in her mind.

She was looking into a wood stove. The fire had burned down to embers and her nose twitched from the faint scent of smoke lingering in the air. Moving her eyes around the room, she noticed the perimeter walls were made from logs. No dividing walls separated the space other than one room with a door. It was open and when she probed inside, she discovered it was a bathroom. Along one wall was a tiny kitchen with open shelving and apartment size appliances. The dining area was comprised of a small wooden table and two chairs placed in the open space between the kitchen and living room area, which had a brown and orange plaid couch and a chair, both facing the fireplace. A bed in a metal bed frame, the mattress covered with a patchwork quilt, was placed along the back wall. The quilt was rumpled as though the bed had been slept in recently. Another table and chairs were placed in front of a large picture window and on the other side was a porch that had been screened. The far edge of the property bordered a lake, frozen now, and a dusting of snow on the evergreen trees and ground sparkled in the sunlight. All of the furniture and furnishings looked like thrift store finds and Annalise realized this was a seasonal cabin. She caught movement outside and spied Violet coming toward the cabin, her arms filled with firewood. She was dressed in jeans and under her puffy winter jacket, she wore an unbuttoned red flannel shirt topping an off-white bulky knit pullover sweater. She had on Maine's signature Bean duck boots and a black knit hat with a pompom on top pulled down over her ears. Stamping her feet first when she entered the porch, she kept her balance with her shoulder braced against the wall as she used her toe for leverage to remove first one boot and then the other, replacing them with a pair of fleece-lined slippers. Despite her arms still being loaded with the firewood, she was able to turn the knob to come into the cabin's main area. Leaning over, she dropped the logs into the wrought iron stand near the wood stove. She put two logs into the stove and poked at them making sparks shoot up from the embers until flames flared around them, before taking off her jacket and hat, tossing them onto an empty chair. She stretched her legs out on the couch and wrapped the blanket around her entire body, more as a source of emotional comfort than protection from the cold.

"You're fine, Violet. They haven't got anything on you. You've burned the clothes and gotten rid of the DNA on the scissors and gloves. You had your gloves on the entire time, so they won't find any of your fingerprints at the hotel. They can't prove it was your car in the parking lot. You saw for yourself the plate number wasn't clear. Just hold it together and wait them out."

The words were spoken as a pep talk that she'd given herself before.

"Probably more than once," Annalise thought.

"You can stay here one more night, but tomorrow you've got

to go home." She was still talking out loud in a conversation with herself. Her mind made up, she scooted down so she was fully reclined, put her head on a pillow, and closed her eyes.

Annalise heard soft snoring and the images dissolved. She blinked several times and then reached for her phone.

"She'll be home tomorrow."

CHAPTER 37

Her sleep had been interrupted with dreams of the police coming to her house with a search warrant in regard to the murder of Benjamin Brooks. When she asked them why they thought it was her, they told her Annalise Jordan had provided them with information that would prove she was Benjamin's killer when they tested her scissors and gloves. Each time she willed herself back to sleep, the dream came again. By morning, she was exhausted, but she had to go home. She needed to get rid of the scissors and the gloves. It didn't make sense. *She'd bleached them. And how would Annalise Jordan even know about them?* The message from her intuition was too strong to ignore, though. She doused the ashes in the wood stove with water and closed up the cabin. All during the two-hour drive back to Glen Lake, the question replayed on a loop in her brain, taunting her. By the time she reached the town line for Glen Lake, she had lost all reason. *I have to pass right by her house on my way home. I'll stop and pretend I'm checking in on her as a follow-up for the craft fair. I want to find out what she said to Nathan, anyway.* She slowed down as she got close to Annalise's house, still on the fence, but her need to know if it was just a nightmare or Annalise might actually be involved won the argument.

Annalise's car was parked in the driveway, but it was the only one. *It's a sign. Pull in.*

She sat for a minute after turning off the car's engine, working up her courage and rehearsing what she would say until a voice in her head urged her to act. *Just do it, Violet. It's now or never.* She walked to Annalise's front door and rang the bell. Making herself stand taller, she breathed in through her nose, and pasted a smile on her face as she peered through the side-light beside the door and saw a figure approaching. A wave of satisfaction flowed through her and she smiled inwardly at the look of surprise on Annalise's face when she opened the door.

"Violet! What a nice surprise. Come in," Annalise said, smiling, but her spidey senses warned her to be cautious.

"I was on my way home, but thought I'd stop by while I was in the neighborhood to see what you thought about the craft fair. Bethany and I want to make sure everyone had a good experience and get their feedback in case we need to make any changes for next year," Violet said, matching Annalise's smile, and stepped inside.

"Oh, of course. I'm glad to help. Let's go in the living room." She gestured to her right and Violet followed her lead, taking a seat in one of the chairs facing the window that looked out onto the road in front of the house. Annalise took a seat on the couch opposite her.

"It's too bad we had that bad press about Benjamin Brooks," Violet said after asking Annalise the safe questions about the fair and what she thought of it from a vendor's perspective. "At least that won't be happening again next year to ruin things." She said it in a matter of fact, dismissive tone. "Have you heard anything more about whether they've caught the person responsible?"

Violet leaned forward toward Annalise as she asked the question, and Annalise sat back involuntarily. Her movement hadn't been threatening, but Violet's eyes were hard... *and dangerous,* Annalise thought. *You'll need to be careful about what you say.*

"No. There hasn't been anything on the news recently. You

know how it is, unless it's something salacious, they lose interest after the first day or two." She kept her tone light. She thought of asking Violet the same question, but decided against it. *Somehow she knows you've been involved in the investigation, or at least suspects.*

"I had the police come to my house a few days ago asking questions. They said they were asking all the vendors and volunteers. Have they come to see you?"

"I have spoken to Detectives Smith and Roberts." Annalise chose her words carefully. "I'd met them before when they were involved on the treasure map case and those men came to my house to find it this past summer."

Violet's eyes narrowed. "You know them?"

"We'd met before, yes."

"Did you tell them I tried to kill Willow Stone when I gave Nathan the peanuts?"

"No! I don't even know what you're talking about."

"Nathan told me you asked about the peanuts. He told you I gave them to him. Do you think I did it on purpose?" her voice was becoming shrill and Annalise knew she was slipping over the edge of sanity.

"I can't imagine why you would want to kill Willow.," she said, keeping her voice calm. "Are you okay, Violet? You seem upset. Maybe some tea would help. I have some herbal tea that always helps me when I'm feeling stressed." She began to stand. She'd left her phone in the kitchen when she went to answer the doorbell. If she could get to it, she could call one of the detectives for help. And warn Liam. They'd made plans and he would be here soon. She didn't want him walking in on this.

"I'm not stressed!" Violet's voice was even louder now.

Annalise sat back down and held Violet's gaze. Violet was the first to look away. She lowered her face and rolled her neck on her shoulders, as she fought to regain her composure. When she raised her head, the smile she gave Annalise chilled her to her core. It was the humorless smile of a madman, or in this case, a madwoman.

"What do you know about the scissors, Annalise?"

The non sequitur threw Annalise off track and her eyes widened but she quickly composed her face in a neutral expression. Not quickly enough, though.

"What. Do. You. Know. About. The scissors?"

She smiled. "I don't have any idea what you're talking about, Violet. What scissors?"

This only enraged Violet more. "Don't play dumb with me. You know what I mean!" she growled. "You told the detectives about the scissors. They've got a search warrant. They're going to search my house!" Violet's hands were clenched on the arms of the chair and Annalise knew she had lost all touch with reality. She leaped up out of her chair and began pacing with her back to Annalise.

Could I make it to the door before she turns around? Annalise thought, estimating how long it would take to cover the distance. As quietly, but quickly, as possible she ran from the couch to the front door and was turning the doorknob when she felt Violet's arms wrap around her. She had Annalise's arms pinned to her body as she dragged her back from the door.

"Where do you think you're going? We're having a conversation here," Violet shrieked in Annalise's ear, making her wince.

She continued pulling Annalise backwards, turning her toward the living room. Before she turned her completely around, Annalise noticed the doorknob turning and the door slowly opening. Through the window she saw Liam's car parked in the driveway. *He's early*, she thought with a mixture of relief and fear. Her first rational thought after Violet grabbed her was to resist, but now her best option might be to allow Violet to take her back to the living room and distract her long enough for Liam to come in. A moment of panic overtook her when she realized Violet might see his car. *Keep her focused on you.*

"Violet, you don't need to do this. Let's just go back and talk about this."

She felt Violet's arms loosen and then release her, but she shoved Annalise in one final show of authority. Annalise stumbled, but recovered her footing and walked quickly to the couch, sitting on the far end facing the door. As she sat, she patted the seat cushion opposite her so that Violet would have her back to the door. "Here, sit down with me. I can see that you're troubled."

Violet glared at her. "You were all against me. You and Sophia, and Fiona, and Bethany. They deserved what I did. And then when Willow told me who her mother is, I knew that's how I could pay Marylou back. If I couldn't do it to her, her daughter was the next best thing. I would have done something to you, too, but you always had your friends around. And that dog." Her voice was cold and her face was contorted with the hatred she was spewing.

"I'm so sorry if we hurt you, Violet. That was so long ago and we were kids. That doesn't make it right, but it's time to let that go," Annalise said in her most soothing tone.

Liam was walking stealthily toward them and he put his finger over his lips when Annalise met his eyes. She focused on Violet again, and was relieved to see that Violet's attention had drifted down and she hadn't caught Annalise looking behind her.

"Easy for you to say," Violet spat, turning her face back up to Annalise. "You're not the one who was told you weren't good enough. I had to just smile and pretend everything was fine while all of you were having a great time and had people fawning over the junk you were selling. And then that photographer. He was going to make me apologize to them. As if I hadn't already been humiliated enough. I didn't mean to kill him but he was going to ruin me. He said he had proof I'd done it. But when I looked on his camera, he didn't have anything. It was all for nothing." Her anger had wound down by then and her words came out quietly. Annalise saw the remorse on her face and by then Liam had reached the couch.

Liam's arms wrapped tightly around Violet. Her eyes opened wide and her mouth gaped open in surprise. As this was happening, they all heard the sound of a car careening into the driveway, its tires spitting up gravel, and a door slammed. Violet struggled to break free of Liam, but he held her even tighter.

"*Let go!*" Violet screamed.

The door swung open and a man in uniform rushed in.

"Deputy Tremblay!" Annalise said, recognizing him, and her shoulders relaxed. He nodded at her in acknowledgement.

"I can take it from here," he told Liam and handcuffed Violet when Liam released her.

"*What are you doing? Take these off me!*" she yelled at Tremblay. "*You have no right doing this. I didn't do anything.*"

"You should call Phil Roberts or Dennis Smith. They'll want to know Violet is here," Annalise told the officer.

"Did she just confess to killing Benjamin Brooks?" Liam asked Annalise.

"I didn't mean to do it. I didn't mean to. It was an accident. I just wanted him to stay away from me so I could delete the photos. That's why I took out the scissors. He was going to take the camera away from me, but I couldn't let him do that until I deleted the pictures of me cutting Sophia's painting. If the sleeping pills had just worked like I thought they would, it wouldn't have been a problem. And do you know what's worse? *They weren't even there!* He lied to me." Violet was sobbing now and tears were streaming down her face.

Officer Tremblay was looking from one to the other, taking it all in. He'd been called to respond to a domestic violence situation, but now there was a murder? Annalise's request to call the homicide detectives made more sense now. He took out his phone and dialed their number.

CHAPTER 38

Phil and Dennis were in an interview room sitting opposite Violet, who was dressed now in a jailhouse uniform.

"We got a search warrant, Ms. Ouellette. When we searched your house, we found the scissors you used when you killed Benjamin Brooks and gloves you were wearing."

Violet's face remained impassive. "Those won't prove anything. They were dirty and I used bleach to clean them. Don't you have scissors and gloves in your house?"

"We do, but ours don't have Benjamin Brooks's blood type on them. It's true you can't get DNA after something's been bleached, but did you know that you can't totally destroy blood with it? It can still be tested for blood type, and the blood the lab found on your scissors wasn't the same as yours. It was, however, his." Phil waited as he let this sink in.

"And then there's the small problem you have of three people hearing you confess to killing him," Dennis followed up. "One of whom is a police officer."

"We found the photos you were looking for. Mr. Brooks had already stored them on the cloud in an encrypted file. They proved you slashed Sophia Peterson's painting. You confessed that's why you were with him that night. To get those photos. That's motive, Ms. Ouellette," Phil added.

"We also found your sleeping pills. They matched what the coroner found when they did the autopsy. Your sleeping pills are a prescription. There were no sleeping pills in the items found in Mr. Brooks's hotel room and no record of him being prescribed sleeping pills." Dennis finished laying out their evidence against her.

Violet's earlier bravado deflated and her body sagged.

"We know this was an accident. Your charges can be reduced if you confess. It won't go well for you if we go to trial. All you have to do is write it out like it happened." Phil slid a pad of paper with a pen on top of it toward Violet.

She only stared at the pad, but Phil and Dennis waited patiently. At last, she pulled it toward her and picked up the pen. When she'd finished her confession, she signed her name, and slid it back toward them, defeated.

CHAPTER 39

The Cozy Quilts Club members were gathered with their spouses and significant others at Annalise's house for a New Year's Eve celebration. The food spread out on her dining room table had been prepared in their usual potluck way, with Annalise adding a few appetizers to the mix. She had pulled more chairs into her living room so they could all be seated together and they each had a plate filled with their selections.

"This is delicious," Jennifer's husband, David said, before popping another mini quiche in his mouth.

Jim gave a thumbs up in agreement, his mouth too full to speak.

"Can you believe we've only known each other six months?" Eva asked.

"Really?" Liam asked, surprised. "You're so close. I thought you'd known each other much longer."

"I have to remind myself it's only been six months, too," Sarah said.

"I just want to say how much I appreciate all of you. I'm not part of your club directly, but the difference it's made in both Sarah's and my lives is remarkable. Before she took the quilting class, she was spending way too much time at work," Ashley began.

"Part of the problem of working from home. You don't have to leave the office, so you lose track of time," Sarah put in.

"That's true, but now, *most* of the time, you stop when you've put in your hours and we get to spend more time together."

"I wasn't sure it was going to work for me with weekly meetings. It's so busy with the kids and all their activities. And with Matthew getting ready to go on to college next year, I thought it was going to be a rough one. But maybe because of that, I'm not nearly as stressed as I thought I'd be because I get a break and a *lot* of venting time," Jennifer said, smiling.

"And I appreciate *that*. It means I'm not the only one who gets the brunt of it all," David said.

"We're glad to share the love," Annalise told him. "I'd begun to isolate more than I should have. It's true I have human interaction with my clients, but that's not the same. I love helping people with their healing but I needed to fill the need to be creative. I was missing that, which is why I took the quilting class. I never imagined it would evolve into what we've built together."

Jim had been quiet, taking it all in.

"I hope you won't take this the wrong way," he looked at Eva before continuing. "When I first met Eva, she hadn't retired yet. She was very excited about the prospect of having more time for her hobbies and couldn't stop talking about it. In a good way," he added when he saw her glaring at him, and winked at her. "That lasted for about six months after she retired. It was obvious that she was missing being around the kids and her fellow teachers. I was beginning to get worried about you, if I'm being honest." This time he was serious and the concern he'd felt was evident. "And then you met these ladies. You talked about how much you appreciate all of them, Ashley, and that's exactly how I feel. I've got my Eva back."

"Well, at least you didn't say you got your *old* Eva back," Eva said. She sounded annoyed but the twinkle in her eyes betrayed her.

"I know better than to even suggest that, my love," he retorted, eliciting chuckles from the others.

"This has probably been the most eventful six months I've ever had. First your Aunt Sadie was murdered, then Annalise had those treasure hunters breaking into her house, Summer Williams was killed in the hit-and-run and we did the Project Linus collection. Eva's lawyer was killed, and now the case with Violet," Sarah said. "I don't know how next year could top that."

Liam's eyes had grown round as he listened to Sarah. He glanced over at Annalise who had been watching his reaction.

"Oh, shoot. I probably shouldn't have said that," Sarah said when she saw Liam's reaction, too. For a moment, she'd forgotten that he was the only one who hadn't known about this before. "Sorry," she said to Annalise.

"I'll fill you in later," Annalise told Liam.

"I can tell you what I'm going to do next," Eva announced. "Quilting Essentials is open tomorrow for all us football widows and I'm going to be there to buy more material. The holiday fabrics are on sale, ladies. Who's with me?"

Three female hands raised, waving excitedly. David and Jim groaned.

"I know exactly what you mean about the downside of working from home, Sarah. I'd been keeping to myself too much, too. When Bethany called me about the craft fair, I almost turned down her invitation, but I'm starting to think it was fate when I decided to accept. When Lise and I started spending time with each other, I was afraid I'd be butting in. Like I said, I thought you'd all been together longer. Instead, you've all welcomed me into your circle and treated me like one of you. I'd like to propose a toast," Liam said, raising his glass. "I think this is even more appropriate given the day we're celebrating. Here's to good friends, new and old. May the coming year bring us even closer!"

"Hear, hear."

"I have one other thing to share with you," Annalise began. "Bethany asked me to co-chair next year's craft fair and I accepted. Better get cracking on your projects, ladies."

This time it was the ladies' turn to groan.

ALSO BY MARSHA DEFILIPPO

Arizona Dreams

Deja vu Dreams

Disillusioned Dreams

A Cozy Quilts Club Mystery series

Follow the Crumbs

Finding the Treasure

Summer's End

Caught in a Spider's Web

Counting Coins

Pulling Out the Hidden Stitches

(Download the story by typing

https://dl.bookfunnel.com/15vlqk2g9h

in your choice of a browser window or use the QR code below.)

ABOUT THE AUTHOR

After retiring from her day job of nearly 33 years, Marsha DeFilippo has embarked on a new career of writing books. She is also a quilter and lifelong avid crafter who has yet to try a craft she doesn't like. She spends her winters in Arizona and the remainder of the year in Maine.

For more information, please visit my website:
marsha defilippo.com

To get the latest information on new releases, excerpts and more, be sure to sign up for Marsha's newsletter.
https://marshadefilippo.com/newsletter

Printed in Great Britain
by Amazon

54607124R00098